Praise for *Naked*

"A dashing, highly original romance rich with alternating perspectives, unexpected swerves, and deftly woven details about art too—Bravo, Betsy Franco!"

—Naomi Shihab Nye, author of *Habibi*

"*Naked* takes us to a familiar place—first, true, unquestionable love—but frames it in an ethereal experience of a fantastical reincarnation meets a coming-of-age story. It shows that love is timeless and ageless; love can heal all wounds, old and new."

—James Franco, author of *Actors Anonymous*, Oscar-nominated actor

"Betsy Franco captures the voice of two people on the verge of adulthood in a way that feels honest and vivid, in a romantic story that's both inventive and classic."

—Gia Coppola, screenwriter, director of *Palo Alto*

D0017729

Naked

Betsy Franco

TYRUS
BOOKS

F+W Media, Inc.

FOR ROBYN

&

CAMILLE B.

Published by
TYRUS BOOKS
an imprint of F+W Media, Inc.
10151 Carver Road, Suite 200
Blue Ash, OH 45242. U.S.A.
www.tyrusbooks.com

Quotes from *Divine Comedy* taken from *Divine
Comedy, Longfellow's Translation, Hell* by Dante
Alighieri, copyright © 2010 by HardPress
Publishing, ISBN 10: 1-4076-0583-6, ISBN 13: 978-
1-4076-0583-8; and *Divine Comedy, Longfellow's
Translation, Purgatory* by Dante Alighieri,
copyright © 2010 by HardPress Publishing, ISBN
10: 1-4076-0586-0, ISBN 13: 978-1-4076-0586-9.

Quotes from Charles Baudelaire taken from *The
Poems and Prose Poems of Charles Baudelaire* by
Charles Baudelaire, copyright © 1919 Brentano's
Publishers.

Excerpt from "A Relationship" copyright © Portia
Carryer, used by permission of the author, all rights
reserved.

ISBN 10: 1-4405-6634-8
ISBN 13: 978-1-4405-6634-9
eISBN 10: 1-4405-6635-6
eISBN 13: 978-1-4405-6635-6

Printed in the United States of America.

10 9 8 7 6 5 4 3 2 1

Library of Congress Cataloging-in-Publication
Data
Franco, Betsy.
  Naked / Betsy Franco.
    p. cm.
  ISBN-13: 978-1-4405-6634-9 (pbk.)
  ISBN-10: 1-4405-6634-8
  ISBN-13: 978-1-4405-6635-6
  ISBN-10: 1-4405-6635-6
  I. Title.
  PS3556.R3325N35 2013
  813'.54--dc23

2013015216

Cover and interior illustrations by Tom Franco.

*This book is available at quantity discounts
for bulk purchases.
For information, please call 1-800-289-0963.*

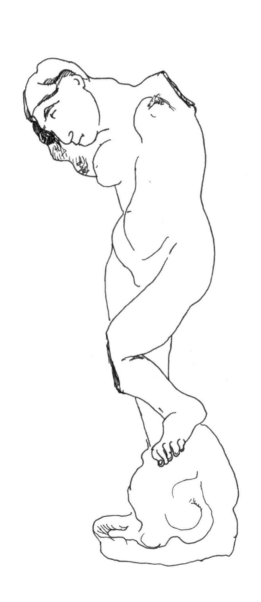

Jesse

*I*t was the statue near the road, the girl looking down, that pulled me into the sculpture garden. Even though Rodin had lopped off her arms and her knee, she still felt complete. Curvy, young. Vulnerable, almost. I walked toward her through the gravel. I had a minute. I was early for my night class.

The bronze of the sculptures looked black in the fading sunlight. The air was still and free of the buzz of mosquitoes. I stood in front of the statue of the girl, called *Meditation*, then reached out and touched her left thigh.

"Shit." I pulled back my hand and sucked on my finger. "What the hell?" I checked to see if my skin had been seared off from the heat of the bronze. It was just red and tender.

The sun had been strong, but not strong enough to heat bronze to a burning point. A nauseous feeling of disorientation took me over. Looking at the statue's bent head, I had the feeling she could see inside me. It was so damned eerie even thinking that, I jerked away from her. I glanced at my watch, half expecting the hands to be twirling counterclockwise.

It was time to get to class. Stanford. What was I thinking? I was going to be the greenest one—guaranteed. Damn, even their summer school was fucking intimidating.

I didn't dare touch the statue again. I blew on my finger, then thought of him. Has he broken me in ways I don't even know yet? Am I going nuts now and don't even realize it? Shit. I left the garden. Wallenberg Hall. Had to find the classroom on campus. Had to get around other people, shake it off.

C___

*I*t started at dusk. A young man entered the garden and lingered by my statue, *Meditation*. I was only a bead of consciousness inside of it, but I could strongly sense his presence. His height, his magnetism, a palpable darkness inside him. After he touched the bronze, he became agitated, then disappeared.

From the moment of his touch, heat permeated my statue, and my consciousness expanded outward, farther and farther, until all at once I left the hollow confines of the sculpture as a moving constellation of lights. I swirled and shifted, until I slowly took a human form, hovering above it. Soundlessly, as subtly as a shiver, I began to materialize into flesh, beginning with my head and breasts, moving down my arms and torso to my legs and feet. I landed on the pedestal, on tiptoe, and grasped the ragged shoulder of the statue. A large white moth that was resting there flew off into the darkness.

The heat permeated my body, awakening my organs. In my chest, my heart vibrated with a terrible ache, as dark memories from the past stirred and forced me to squeeze my eyelids shut against the pain.

A blast of light burst inside me, a feeling of wild anticipation that made my vision blur, and settled into an ebb and flow of emotion—hope and disappointment, joy and sadness, tranquility and anger—like a wave receding and crashing on a beach.

Shivering, then shuddering, shook my body and made my teeth chatter. I leaned my hip firmly against the statue for balance and hugged myself, hoping the warmth of my arms would settle the spasms. I pulled air into my chest and let it out slowly, trying to calm myself.

Under my hand, I felt the undeniable rhythm of a heartbeat.

I had lived a life before . . . I felt it. But the soft skin on my hands, my vitality, told me I was young again. I explored my face with my fingers: high cheekbones, strong nose, full lips. I touched my breasts; my arms and thighs, strong and smooth; the curve of my waist; my rounded hips. Into my hands, I gathered my long dark-brown hair and clutched it tightly. I was young, for certain. Eighteen? Nineteen?

Below me I could see the ground, a white surface. Extending one leg downward, and then the other, I lowered myself until coarse pebbles bit into my toes. Once down, I slowly circled the statue, shielding my naked body with my hands. From the front, I could see its beautiful asymmetry and how it flowed into the shape of a question mark. The statue was a question and an answer all in one.

My gaze suddenly settled on objects in the distance, and I looked around, my eyes flitting here and there.

I am outside. Naked! Am I in danger?

I hugged myself tightly, crisscrossing my arms in front of my nakedness, madly searched the darkness, and listened for the sound of another living being. No one.

But there were strange, motionless human shapes around me.

I was in a garden of sorts, filled with a family of statues, each an island of its own surrounded by white gravel. Those to my right were blacker than the night sky, but I knew they were bronze. I knew sculpture. I could feel it in my fingers. There was a small comfort in that.

Two of the statues were seated, one was reaching skyward, another was on its back, two more were perched on tall pedestals. To my left, giant bronze gates were illuminated, filled with the contorted faces of clamoring figures. I knew all the sculptures I could see, but did not know why. I felt a sharp ache again around my heart. And a tremor of panic.

Mon dieu.

Who am I?

Who was I?

J peered through the sliding door. The chairs inside the classroom were pushed to the left. There were spotlights dotting the black ceiling, a camera on a tripod to the right, and two standing lights with umbrellas over them.

I walked in, avoiding the wires snaking around the floor. "This Performance Art?"

"Enter at your own risk," the teacher said. Marc Stein. He was young, bearded, wore a baseball cap. A Steven Spielberg wannabe. His bio said he'd gotten his work into festivals.

I held out my one-page write-up exploring a possible topic for a project.

"Keep it." He waved me off, continued fussing with a computer. "There'll be a lot more where that came from. You'll hand in your whole journal later."

Suddenly an image appeared on a screen on the wall, captured by the camera. I almost didn't recognize myself. My gangly body, my confused eyes. I moved out of range of the camera lens.

"Hi, I'm Lisa." A girl my height hovered beside me as I folded my paper and pushed it into my backpack. Tight jeans, wavy blonde hair to her shoulders. A silver top with no sleeves. Her brown eyes and dark eyebrows looked interesting with her hair.

"Jesse."

"You ever taken anything from him before?" she asked.

"Nope."

"I heard he can see through people, really get them to move places."

"O-kay."

I sat down and noted each person who entered, pretending to take an interest in my crinkled syllabus.

Lisa slipped into a folding chair next to me, smiling and staring at me longer than she needed to. I thought about Rachel at Columbia summer school. Was she smiling at guys like that, even though we'd made a pact to keep it going between us? Hell, we'd gone together for a year. And it wasn't like we'd broken up or anything. But long distance relationships had a bad rep for a reason.

Lisa's voice interrupted my nosedive. "Haven't seen you around the drama department."

"I don't actually go here."

"I'm hoping I have to drop out of Stanford early because I'm discovered." Her grin showed off her perfectly white teeth.

"Sounds good. I'm hoping for any break, any time."

People filtered in. I was probably the youngest. There's a look to a college student. Hadn't put my finger on what it was before Marc Stein started in, "Want to get going right away with some improv stuff. Everyone in the center of the room and let's get moving around. Don't touch each other. Focus on the spaces between you. Your body is your instrument in performance, so it needs a vast repertoire. Focus on relaxing as much as you can."

We circled the room, weaving in and out of each other's way, feet shuffling on the linoleum floor. Marc called out scenarios: "You're suspicious of everyone. How would you carry yourself?" That was easy. Fuck. We all felt that way already. At least, I did. Then he changed it up. "You just got a new outfit, and you're feeling flirtatious."

Everyone was checking each other out, eyes flashing, bodies more fluid. A girl with short spiked hair brushed me as she passed. One guy— someone had called him Tito—looked kind of relatable. Other than that, I was a fish out of the aquarium. I had to remember I wasn't in the class to make friends.

"No mugging," Marc Stein said. "I want to see who you are, want to strip you to the bone, to the marrow. Don't worry. I've got your best interests in mind." He smiled and a couple people laughed. "Now, turn to your left and pair up with that person. Find a place in the room. Think of an event in your life that made a significant impact on you, and tell your partner about it. We'll be getting to know each other intimately, so might as well start now."

This girl with short brown hair nodded at me, and we found some chairs in the corner. Her name was Alenka. She said she was from Russia.

"You can start," I said. "I'm not sure what to use yet."

I watched her bright red lips and green eyes as she talked. "My friends and I were on this hike in the wilderness, when, suddenly, we found we were lost." She told me how they wandered for a whole day, way off track, and nearly ran out of food—only had a few small candies to divvy up. She said they were normal college students, but were instantly stripped down to their barest survival instincts, like animals, each person focused on himself.

I didn't have any stories like that. When she stopped, I quickly picked through my life, discarding most of the events that made a difference. Hell, I didn't even know these people. Then I remembered Jasper. That was safe.

"I had this dog named Jasper, a brown and black mutt," I told Alenka. She barely blinked as she listened. "Even though we moved around a lot, I could always count on him." I described what it was like to enroll in a new school every year or so. "Then one night, when I was in middle school, Dad came into the kitchen and said our next place was going to be an apartment—nothing he could do about it—and they didn't allow pets of any kind."

"One more minute," Marc Stein said. "Then go back to your seats. You're going to tell us the other person's story as if you were them." Lots of buzzing in the room.

"We had to give Jasper to another family."

My mind started scrambling to piece together Alenka's story. Where did she say they were? They'd taken the train to some deserted area, or something.

Marc Stein set up a chair in front of the camera. "When it's your turn, look at me while you're talking. Don't worry about the camera. Remember it's your friend, if you let it be."

Tito sat down next to me, and his partner, a shy Asian American girl, told his story first. He apparently jacked a car with some older friends when he was fourteen.

"That's heavy, man," I said.

"Yeah, it's a miracle I'm fucking here to tell the tale. After six months in juvie and a couple years of community service, I'd had it with that shit."

"You go to Stanford?"

"Holding on by my fingernails. You?"

"I'm headed for Chapman. Student loans up the ass."

"Cool. I hear ya."

"Jesse, your turn." Marc Stein motioned me to the hot seat.

When I told Alenka's story, I honestly felt some of the desperation she'd gone through. But it was awkward, in the playback, to see how the camera knew when I was real or not. I couldn't fool it. Every twitch, every movement of my eyes, every crease on my forehead, every detail of how I held my body, every doubt I had—the camera picked it all up.

"Jesse, there were a few truthful moments," Marc Stein said, "but you don't need to force it so much. The camera can see through you—through your eyes. Occurs to me you've mostly been on stage. Relax into it more. With film, it's an intimate conversation."

Before we left, he answered questions about the performance art piece we were going to have to create and film. "You should have already started a journal. I want to see how you come up with the concept for your piece and how it develops."

"But how can we know what to do if the class just started?" Tito asked. Thank God for Tito. Everyone else was afraid to ask.

"Jump in. Take chances. Be original." That's all Marc Stein would say.

After class, I decided to head back to the garden and the statue, to show myself I wasn't nuts. I was in a lot better shape now that I'd navigated one class. I could keep the pace—I'd taken drama for four solid years. I felt reasonably comfortable in front of people. More comfortable shedding my skin and climbing into a role than being myself. But maybe that would come.

Besides, I was thinking more seriously about using the sculpture garden as a jumping-off place for my performance art piece.

*B*y a large juniper bush to my right, the crunch of gravel.

I clung to the statue, tensed like an animal, and peered through the darkness, in the direction of the sound. The shape of a man. He stood by a bench. Facing away. He lowered his shoulder to pull off a pack.

I am naked!

I slipped behind the pedestal. The moonlight and the circular lights coming from the ground lit him from above and below. His body was muscular, but not overly so. I startled at the shape of his hands and fingers.

Rodin? I held my breath. The man's head turned and he seemed to meet my eyes.

No. He was not Rodin. But why would I think this? Was I mad?

I steadied myself against the statue and looked more closely, limp with confusion. Was he the one at dusk? The one who touched my statue?

A musical sound. He reached in his pocket, pulled out a small, flat object, and cradled it in his palm, staring at it for a few seconds. "Errr," he groaned and jammed it back into his pocket. On the back of his neck, just above his collar, I saw what looked like a small tattoo in a dark ink.

He turned and slumped onto the bench, sighing and running his fingers through his brown hair, which looked as thick as molten metal and nearly covered the tops of his ears. I studied him. He did not seem to be someone to run from. I could not be sure.

The ground lights shining on his cheekbones gave him a sculptural look, as did the two furrows deepening between his eyebrows. His nose was classic, with a slight bump. He wore a black shirt with a figure on it and short brown pants that came above the knees, with many pockets.

His legs were covered with dark hairs, and on his feet were sandals that were very worn, with a strap between the toes.

I had a strong urge to call to him, to study his strong features more closely, to run my fingers along his tanned face.

What was I thinking? I did not even know this man. Nothing made sense. Nothing.

When he raised his eyes, I twisted sideways behind the pedestal, trying to hide every part of my naked body. Had he seen me?

The music again. I peeked around the statue as he pulled out the small object once more and stared at it. "Fuck 'im. Can't leave me alone," he muttered under his breath. He grimaced, threw the object on the gravel, and rubbed hard at his temples.

English . . . he speaks English. Coarse English. And I seem to understand it, though it is not native to me.

He looked up again. His eyes were black or dark brown, and they were deep. And haunted? We were connected. I saw something in him that I should not be seeing, something private. For certain, he did not know I was studying him, but I could not stop watching as he leaned down for the flat object and grabbed it as if he would crush it. A small indistinguishable sound came from his lips—I almost felt as if I had made the noise. I wanted to scream, to shout, but I remained mute. He jammed the object into his pack, causing some papers to fall out, which he hastily gathered. Shrugging on his pack, he began to walk off into the shadows, planting each foot heavily on the gravel. Then he hesitated and looked back.

Was he looking for me?

*I*t was dark after class, and the sculpture garden looked like a different place. Each statue was lit from below—very dramatic, and a little eerie. From the minute I arrived, I sensed I wasn't alone. I thought I saw someone at the edge of my vision, but then, the sculptures were very realistic. And the damn phone calls had put me in a weird headspace.

As I turned to leave, I looked back to make sure no one was there.

"Do not go. Who are you?" It was a female voice. I spun around, the gravel growling under my feet.

"Who said that?" I searched the dark.

"I am here."

She seemed to be behind the meditation statue. A strong accent.

"Do not come close," she said.

"Okay." I stretched my neck and squinted in her direction.

"I must have your shirt."

"What? This?" I pulled at the front of my T-shirt. I almost laughed, but not because it was funny.

"Please." As she shifted position behind the statue, my eyes found hers, and I could see a bit of shoulder, a white hip flickering on the edge of the bronze.

"You're serious, aren't you? Are you okay?" This girl, this woman sounded young. Around my age.

"I must have the shirt now."

"Well, uh. O-kay. If it'll help." I slowly pulled it up and slipped it over my head. I knew she must be staring at me. I felt strange about the whole thing, and self-conscious about the scar near my rib, but it was probably too dark to see it.

I bit my lip to stifle a half-smile. With an odd sense of gravity, I placed my shirt in front of the statue like an offering, then lingered, my eyes darting around despite myself, trying to catch a glimpse of her.

She motioned me away with her hand, and I obeyed, walking backwards. A squeak of relief escaped from her mouth as she slipped on the shirt.

"So, what's going on?" I asked, arms crossed in front of me, hands in my pits. Awkward. "What happened?"

"This is what I want to know. What happened?" she asked, her voice firm. Holding the statue with one hand and keeping her legs hidden, she looked out at me. Her hair was very long, and dark. "And why are you here tonight? You were in the garden two times, no?"

"Been keeping track of me, huh?" I was sorry about being a wiseass right after the words came out. "Actually, I'm just here to do some research on Rodin." I inched forward. "Why are you here?"

"Do you know why I am here?" Her voice was urgent.

"What? Listen, this is pretty strange, don't you think? How would I . . . ?" I peered through the dark. "Are you all right? I don't think you should be out here tonight by yourself. Are you wasted?"

"I do not wish to waste this life," she insisted.

I laughed softly. "O-kay. How about this? Let me walk you back to your dorm." I moved to my right, to get a better view of her, to pick up some cues, but she edged around to the opposite side of the statue.

"You are the only person, tonight, in this garden with me," she said. "This is *significatif*, uh, significant. I think you know why I am here." She stared at me, waiting for an answer. I could hear her uneven breathing.

"French accent, right? Look, I think you'll feel better if you sleep this off." I tried to keep my voice low and unthreatening. "Seriously, you weren't raped or anything, were you?"

"No. I was *réincarné*. I was reborn."

"A born-again? Oh, okay. So that's what this is about."

"I do not understand."

"Never mind. Really. Just keep the shirt."

"Thank you."

"Actually, that happens to be my favorite Iggy Pop shirt. Don't mean to be possessive, but could I meet you back here sometime? That way I'd know you were okay, too."

"I will be here, always."

"Suure. Um, could you please let me drop you somewhere?"

"I am fine. You may go, but please return."

"This whole thing isn't adding up. I'm only leaving you here if you honestly think you'll be safe."

She nodded.

"Okay, then." As I slowly headed toward the road, the straps of my pack against my bare skin, I glanced back at her. I could have sworn she wanted me to stay, even though she was telling me to go.

*I*t was so difficult to allow him to leave. When his eyes met mine for the last time, he did not look away for longer than I expected.

After he disappeared from view, I heard the roaring sound of a machine, then it was quiet, save for the striking of a clock in the distance. Ten times.

I did not know him. But already I missed him. I pictured the look of his eyes, and I resonated deeply with the darkness behind them.

You must not think in this way about a man who is a stranger to you, I warned myself. With all my will, I tried to stop the parade of thoughts in my mind.

There was a touch of warmth left in the night air, which was a blessing. I crouched behind the pedestal, arms around my legs, my hair covering me. My body was still vibrating from sharing the space with him. When it quieted, I scanned the garden. No one was approaching from any direction. The only sound was the loud silence of the night's darkness filling the air and touching the earth.

I forced myself from my hiding place and headed for the wooden bench near the statue of Orpheus, who was reaching his arms for the sky. This area was the most sheltered from view. The gravel dug into my toes and heels as I walked.

Out of the corner of my eye, I spotted something blue. Pulling the shirt down over the tops of my thighs, I reached into the unruly branches of the giant juniper bush beside me and grabbed it. A light blue sock, slightly tattered. I pulled it onto my right foot and felt the warmth. It was something. Not much, but something.

Settled on the bench, hidden by a large, rambling tree, I sat with a straight spine, palms turned upward on my thighs, and meditated. It was something I understood, the one thing I remembered from being within the statue. But I could not keep my eyes shut for long. My awareness returned to the garden again. The wooden slats of the bench pressed against my legs, and my stomach fluttered with anxiety.

It did nothing for me to think again and again of how I came to be here. I rubbed my limbs for warmth, and tucked my bare foot underneath me. I had to sleep.

To my left, a mockingbird called, "Dee dee dee, cheru, cheru." I wanted to think it was speaking to me. In a row of tall trees that divided the garden in two, I spotted the bird. It took flight, soared in front of me with a whir of wings that startled me, then flew across a narrow cement road to an open field. Pushing myself to navigate the blanket of darkness, I followed the bird and explored the large field for bedding. It was mostly bare earth, prickly shrubs, and trees of odd shapes that loomed up at me when I came close to them, but scattered throughout were clumps of dried grasses, mixed with twigs and debris. I pulled at them blindly and gathered armfuls.

Beneath the giant juniper bush, I piled the grasses to form a nest. I crawled under the bush, avoiding the sharp branches as best I could, and curled up to sleep, my limbs close to my body for warmth.

Lying still, I could feel the memories of my past life forming slowly and slyly, one tiny image attaching to another, the beginning of a tapestry appearing stitch by stitch. And with it came a feeling. Of fear—so intense it scratched and bit at my insides.

Letting the fear in even for an instant created a tiny opening to a part of my memory that was deeply buried, locked away. I shuddered and stared up into the branches of the juniper, then peered through them to find my statue.

Why was I here?

———— • ◆ • ————

Crunch, clank. I startled awake and grabbed at the grasses of my bedding. I was still alive.

The sky above me was a bright, cloudless blue. A man with a mustache was emptying the garbage from metal receptacles on the far side of the garden of statues.

Another container of garbage stood next to my juniper bush. My heart beat as quickly as a bird's. The man would be here very soon. I crawled out from under the juniper, scraping my leg on a branch, and scanned the area beyond the benches. Behind them was a circle of low bushes. I crept over and ducked down in their center.

Once the man disappeared from view and I could no longer hear the clank of his cart, I came back out and sat on my bench. The thick strands of my hair draped my arms and shoulder blades like a shawl. It was just as well I had no barrette to clip them up. I sat carefully with my legs drawn under me, praying no one would take notice of me.

As I watched the sun rising between the trees in the field and the palette of the sky grew brighter, I felt more exposed and more alone. How do I survive here? For solace, I looked to my statue, *Meditation*, glowing in the morning sun, then surveyed the other statues in the garden, all wordless and still. My breathing began to even out as a group of a dozen people entered the garden, led by a woman with smooth gray hair to her shoulders. Quietly, I moved to the shadow of a tree.

"Welcome to Stanford's Rodin Sculpture Garden. Gather round." The woman started at the bronze gates, where I could hardly hear her, then led the group to *Meditation*.

My statue.

She seemed to be a guide. I stayed at a distance, but took in every word.

"Camille Claudel, Rodin's muse, inspired this beautiful sculpture," the guide said. "Walk around it for a moment. Go ahead. Touch it."

I covered my mouth and supported myself against the tree's trunk as the garden spun before me. I drew in my breath and let it out, grasping at the rough trunk. Pieces of bark fell to the ground.

Camille Claudel. The name echoed in my head, over and over, as if calling to me.

"Everyone on this side, please," the guide said, herding the visitors to the front of the statue.

I touched my face, my nose, my eyes, my mouth. Dizziness again, as I floated from the past to the present and back. My heart beat inside my head.

I must be Camille! I am Camille.

The guide spoke more loudly. "Rodin considered this meditation sculpture to be both graceful and powerful. *The Kiss*, Rodin's best known, was also inspired by Camille."

People on the tour began whispering about *The Kiss*. When the guide lowered her voice, they stopped their private chatter and leaned toward her. "Exactly one hundred years ago, in 1908," she said, "Camille Claudel appeared in public for the last time. After that, she lost a part of herself, her essence, or so people said."

My body was cold and feverish at the same time. I closed my eyes.

"I never heard that about Camille," an older woman said.

"It's my pet theory," the guide said, her eyes twinkling, "that Camille haunts this garden." She laughed lightly at her own words and moved to the next statue. "Follow me."

My heart ached, and I held my chest firmly with my hand. Slowly, I moved to my bench. What was this part of myself I lost?

I did not hear anything more, though the group gathered quite near me. Staring out into the garden, my past came drifting back to me in pieces:

Rodin was my teacher.

My body told me more:

He was my lover.

In my mind, I saw a glimmer of myself standing with Rodin in Paris. When I met him, I was eighteen.

I seem to be eighteen again.

"*Y*ou up, honey? When do you have to be at work? It's getting late." The sound of Mom's voice from downstairs just barely reached my bedroom.

I rubbed my eyes awake with my palms. The clock said 10:24. Shit. I grabbed the schedule next to the lamp. My name was in the middle of the page, along with Jim's. Thank God. I rolled back on the pillow. Eleven o'clock start, then straight to class.

Once I was upright, which took some doing, I stumbled around the room, trying to avoid books and weights, kicking clothes out of the way. I sniffed at my clothes, and threw on some shorts and a shirt that still seemed wearable.

Rachel looked back at me from a photo on my long wooden desk. Someone had taken the picture at a film festival. She was gesturing to me with one hand and running her fingers through her short, blunt-cut hair with the other. I had my arm around her shoulder, her red hair fiery next to my black hoodie.

All wrapped up in the Beats, her last text had said. *Class even meets in some of their old haunts. Howz yr class? Started yet? Making friends here. Some guy knows more abt Ginsberg than anyone so far. U would love it here.*

Friends? Fuck. She didn't make friends that easily when we first got together. Hid behind her academics. We joked about her being neurotic and pushy, about how being with me had loosened her up a lot—that's what she'd said, anyway. By the time the year was over, we were bonded at the hip. And my grades had gone up.

I wanted to tell her about class. But it seemed like all she really cared about was New York now. The big city suited her. Good for her, but it left me feeling sick.

I texted back. *Teacher is young brilliant type. Wants us to be ourselves instead of losing ourselves in a role. Might do something on Rodin. Miss talking to you. Whens a good time? Wish youd gone to summer school here. Being long distance from you sucks.*

After I wrote her, I searched online for a performance art piece Marc Stein had mentioned. Couldn't figure out the spelling of the woman's name. Abromo . . . something. I was thinking of proofing my first paper for the class, now that I realized how tough Marc Stein could be, but I couldn't find it anywhere in my backpack. Dumped everything out, and still no paper.

"Dammit."

"Do you have enough time for breakfast?" Mom called from downstairs.

"Maybe an egg sandwich? To go. Thanks."

I searched for my paper on the computer to print it out again. That's when the car door slammed. The muscles in my jaw clamped.

The front door banged. Some talking in the living room. Footsteps up the stairs. The bedroom door opened, and there he was, in his blue gas station uniform, back from the night shift. His blond-gray hair stuck straight up. His badge was still in place on the front of his shirt. *Manager.*

"Wasting your time again, huh?" Dad said.

"No, it's for class."

"Deposited your check?"

I nodded and kept my eye on his hands. He moved closer to my desk chair. Three feet from me now. He took a step toward me, and I flinched. He just stood there and laughed.

I tensed, waiting for more.

He stayed where he was, rolling his shoulder, straightening his back, smirking at me—making me jump each time like a monkey on a string. Playing me.

He chuckled again as he headed out of the room, running his hands over his crew cut, shaking his head.

When I could hear him talking downstairs, I got up, shut the door without a sound, and punched the air with both fists, over and over again, until my jaw hurt from clenching it so hard.

No matter what I did, I triggered something in him. Maybe I stood for everything he couldn't do after I was born. How was I going to take it for the rest of the summer? Even for one more day?

Motherfucker.

J guessed it was midmorning from the strength of the sun. I was pulled from deep within myself by the sound of bustling and laughter. A group of young people filled the garden, tossing their packs in a heap onto the gravel near *Orpheus*. Their voices invigorated me. All of them wore light brown shorts and shirts, even the girls, and their feet were bare. Many of the girls had short hairstyles like the boys.

These students seemed to be wearing only undergarments. I stared at them and could not stop, then laughed to myself because I was wearing less. In public.

"Now that you've changed into your dance clothes, let's begin," said a woman whose black hair was wrapped loosely in a bun. Their teacher. "Come to *The Gates of Hell* for inspiration."

I waited and watched until all the students had gathered at the far end of the garden. With my eye on the group, I jumped up and began scavenging through the packs closest to me. I slipped a short skirt made of rough blue material over my hips. Under that, I quickly pulled on black tights that stopped at the ankle. An orange sock peeked out of a shoe. I snatched it and put it on my bare foot.

Standing with my feet together, I wiggled my toes. Blue and orange. Complementary colors.

"Contemplate, meditate on each sculpture," said the teacher. "Then pick one statue for your own. Allow yourself to feel the statue in your body, completely."

A few students turned around to survey the garden. I dodged behind the juniper and held my breath.

"I am not quite finished," the teacher said.

When the students looked back at her, I resumed my search. A coral top without sleeves and a lacy top with short sleeves were at the top of two packs. I pulled them both out. Behind the juniper, I yanked off the black shirt, slipped the tops over my head and covered them with the shirt. Then I searched the bags again. I found short pants that came to mid-thigh and soft, stretchy shoes that looked like lavender ballet slippers, which I tossed under the juniper so the students would not spot them on my feet. My last discovery was a hooded gray sweater, for the nights and cool mornings. I pushed that under the bush as well.

I had several outfits now, but I knew I did not dress this way ever before—like a boy. I knew it for certain when a memory-image filled me: My hands piling my long hair onto my head and clipping it there with a tortoiseshell clasp, the bottom of a cream-colored skirt almost touching the ground.

I was pulled back to the present by the teacher's voice in the sculpture garden. "Spend time with your sculpture. Feel it in your body. Feel its volume. Use all your senses. What would it be like if you were that sculpture? How would you move? What would you feel?"

The students shuffled through the gravel. A boy sat with his fist under his chin, copying a pose from the bronze gates. Two boys picked tortured poses from the gates as well. Three girls chose the statue near the front of the garden, three standing figures, heads touching and bent. Another lay on her back in the stiff pose of a statue one of the students called *Martyr*. And one picked *Meditation*. She posed well as my statue, with just the right tilt of her head.

A student with short-cropped hair, who looked like an elf, came near my bench and contemplated *Fallen Caryatid with Stone*.

"You in the class?" she asked.

"No, I am not," I tugged down my black shirt, hoping none of the new clothes were hers.

"I hope I'm not in your way," she said as she settled on the gravel in front of the statue she had chosen.

"It is interesting, what you are doing with the statues. Continue, please. But where am I?"

"I'm not sure what you mean."

I tried to calm my voice, to cover over my desperation. "What is the address of this place?"

"Oh, it's part of Stanford University."

"Stanford University?"

"I guess you'd say it's in Stanford, California."

"Thank you." A swishing filled my ears. California. I lived in Paris, in my other life. But now I was in California?

The teacher's voice carried through the garden, "Once you've chosen your statue, think: Where have I been? What is my history? What is my name?"

I pinched at the flesh on my arms until it throbbed. History. I need to build a new history, if that is even possible. And I must have a name, a new name. When I glanced around for inspiration, I spotted a piece of paper wedged next to the leg of the bench beside mine. I retrieved the paper, dusted off the dirt, and read the uniform black type.

July 1

Jesse Lucas

Research/Topic Search for performance piece

I'm thinking Rodin's sculptures might be the center of my performance piece. The possibilities for filming at night are amazing, especially *The Gates of Hell*. I've got no idea what the big concept will be, but researching Rodin's life can't hurt—just see where it leads me.

Auguste Rodin was one of those guys who never caught a break early on. Artists were supposed to go to the École des Beaux-Arts, but he could never pass the entrance exam for sculpture—didn't fit the mold. How ironic is that? Depressed the hell out of him, but maybe it was lucky. He avoided years of neoclassical training, and it puts him in good company: Steinbeck couldn't pass freshman English, Tarantino dropped out of high school, Spielberg was turned down by USC film school three times.

How did Rodin become such a rebel, in spite of being the son of a son-of-a-bitch (not confirmed) policeman and a seamstress from the country? How does someone evolve into an artist with a background like that? genes? predestination? ambition stoked by unhappiness?

Correction: I was wrong about Rodin's father being an SOB. It turns out he wrote encouraging letters to his son advising him to keep up his energy, not to fall into "slackness," "effeminacy," or depression. Told him he'd be such a famous sculptor one day, people would remember him long after he was dead.

I'm guessing/hoping you don't need that kind of support to make it as an artist—so many were misunderstood. But does it add something to your work? Picasso's father thought he was a genius, Daniel Day-Lewis's father was poet laureate. Michael Jackson was encouraged *and* beaten. It's confusing, but no matter what, Rodin was damn lucky to have the father he had. Research next: Camille Claudel—how does she fit into Rodin's life?

This person writes of Rodin. Of me! His language is coarse, and he needs to research more deeply. He knows so little. Could it be the young man who said he studied Rodin? I folded the paper until it was small enough to slip into my skirt pocket.

I still needed to find a name. Not Rodin or Auguste, although they were powerful. Not Camille. No, I must certainly start again.

The rest of the morning, I observed people, some crisscrossing the garden on their way to somewhere else, some stopping to spend time with the statues. Nearly everyone was scantily clothed. We were all like the models in the studio of an artist. If we took off only a few pieces of clothing, we would be naked. I smiled at my own joke.

As a respite, I meditated for hours until my stomach growled and churned, and I could not stop watching people drop food into the garbage cans. Saliva gathered in my mouth. Was I truly so desperate? I vowed to myself I would not eat garbage. It was disgusting.

But as the day wore on, I found myself leaning over the garbage like a wild animal. I dug through the waste, gingerly at first. A banana peel, an empty bottle made of soft material, unlike glass. A transparent container with bits of chicken. I dug deeper. A half-eaten sandwich!

On my bench, I ate my first meal. The chicken was tough but tasty, and the sandwich had bits of sausage, a pleasant surprise. The food renewed my energy, and I turned back to my body to study myself in more detail, finding blue bruises on both knees and both shoulders. As those limbs were missing or chipped away on my statue, it made some sort of strange sense. My torso was untouched, and on my legs, the skin was taut and smooth, with muscles almost like those of a dancer. My breasts stood out, not large but admirable. I spent a long time combing my fingers through my tangled hair.

People continued to pass through the garden, but I was mainly alone until midday, when a white-haired man arrived. He hobbled onto the gravel, clutching a newspaper, and lowered himself onto the bench near *Meditation*. I observed him at first, but then my loneliness gripped me, and I made my way slowly to the bench kitty-corner to his and settled back. The shape of his eyes and a softness around them reminded me of someone—he looked kind. At intervals, I glanced up at him and noticed his skin was dry and wrinkled, and thin strands of hair lay limp on his head. He unfolded the newspaper, he dozed and read, he muttered something to himself. The man seemed to be near the end of his life.

How much time did I have? It could be minutes more, or a whole lifetime. I shivered, even with the sun warming my shoulders. How long did I have to find this part of myself I had lost? And how was I meant to do it? Anger flared in my chest. I breathed as deeply as I could, trying to ward off panic. For that moment, I knew the best thing was to sit with this old gentleman and try not to scare him away.

I crossed my legs, leaned back, and read a *Welcome* brochure about a museum—someone had left it on the bench. Over my shoulder was a grand sandstone building that was probably the museum. It was open late on Tuesdays, and there were galleries of art from Asia, Europe, Greece, Egypt, Oceania. Oceania? There was Native American art and a whole gallery for Rodin. Hmm, they revered Rodin. As I studied the maps, I felt as if the old man and I were doing something together. On my third reading of the brochure, I looked up and he looked up.

We smiled at each other, and I found myself speaking out loud. "Hello."

"*Buenos días*," he said, bowing his head slightly.

It made my body relax to be spoken to so gently. Who did he remind me of?

A memory from the past made me shut my eyes: Two faces. Me, and someone near to my age. My brother. That was it. We were laughing. Then an image of my packed valise, his teary eyes, my dry eyes, as I stepped up into a carriage. Perhaps I had been cold—perhaps I had let go of loved ones too easily then.

I opened my eyes and stared at the muscular statue of *Eve*—all of the names were returning to me. She brought me back to the garden, to the present. After the old man rose, glanced at me, and tottered off, I picked up his newspaper. It was in Spanish, but I could guess at the date on the top of the page. *3 de Julio de 2008*. Two thousand eight. The newspaper brushed my legs and landed at my feet as I let go of it to wrap my arms around myself and dig my fingernails into my flesh.

*S*econd day of class, Tito was outside the room with an iPod.

"What're you listening to?"

"Dubstep."

"You're shittin' me? I love that electronic stuff. Bassnectar, Deadmau5 . . . ."

"Tiësto."

We shuffled into the room behind Lisa and Claire. Marc Stein was brushing his teeth and spitting into a bowl. Then he flossed meticulously. No one said a word. We all looked at each other.

"No time to brush at home?" Tito blurted out.

"He's got to be doing some kind of performance art, right?" Lisa said. She looked at me for confirmation.

"Yeah, I guess . . . . Should be an interesting class," I whispered to Tito.

"Some of you asked why we did improv last class," Marc Stein said. "If you read the class description, you'd understand that the purpose of any acting or improv we do is to push you out of your individual ruts in the road—the ones you follow by default."

We all watched as he shook the contents of the bowl into the trash.

"So, I asked you to wear something you would never wear, to class and for several hours leading up to class. I see some of you complied and some didn't."

It looked like Halloween. I was wearing a wifebeater shirt with a bandanna around my head, a fake tattoo of a dragon on one arm and a Celtic symbol on the other. I'd put it all on after work. Walked around

Stanford before class. If I'd paraded around at work like that, I'd have never lived it down. Some skinny, tall guy was wearing a tutu over his shorts. Lisa had on a conservative tan suit, and her hair was poofed way out all over her head. It didn't budge when I touched it.

"Got the outfit from my aunt," she whispered. "Like your look, Jesse."

"Claire, tell us about your experience," Marc Stein said. He stopped beside her and gestured for her to stand opposite the camera.

"My parents have always put a lot of restrictions on how I dress. So I bought this T-shirt and wore it around all day."

The shirt had *tits and ass* on the front and *I like it like that* on the back. Claire seemed just the opposite. She was Asian American, or at least partially. Had been very buttoned up the first class.

"Lots of people did a double-take and raised their eyebrows at me," she said. "It was the first time I haven't felt invisible."

"Risk-taking. That's what it's all about," Marc Stein said. Then he pointed to me. I replaced Claire in front of the class and the camera.

A queasy feeling in my stomach. I let out my breath, the way they taught us in drama, and dove in. "I'd never wear this. People I passed were looking at me like I'd straggled onto campus by mistake. Or like I was a blue-collar worker here to repair something. It pissed me off that people were looking down on me—'course, that could have been just my take on it. It was more the adults than students." Damn, I sounded like a two-year-old.

"But how much of a risk was it?" Marc Stein asked. "We can all appreciate that you have decent abs. But you already know you're good looking. Now if you had a gut, that would be different." My neck felt warm. "Showing off your body was hardly a stretch. More vulnerability mandatory in your corner, Jesse. Play it safe, and you're guaranteed not to grow. I'm sure that's not what you want."

I slunk down into my seat and tried to suck it up as Marc Stein alternately cut people apart or approved of them. I knew he was right about me. Last spring, my drama teacher told me the same: "You just need to go deeper. Be fearless. Push the envelope, Jesse, and you'll go places you want to go."

After class, I yanked off the bandanna and slipped a white T-shirt over the wifebeater. Lisa exited beside me, and we walked to the oval of grass. It was surrounded by parked cars from all the night students.

"It's not Performance Art 101," she said. "I think he hates me."

"He's tough."

"I took a year off before college, studied acting in San Francisco, and this is still hard."

"Oh, yeah? Good to know." I laughed. "Thought it was just me."

When we arrived at the path leading to the sculpture garden, I stopped. "Hey, this's where I head off."

"Peeing in the bushes?" she laughed.

"Not really. I might do something on Rodin for class."

"Can I walk with you?"

I nodded, mainly because I didn't know exactly how to say *no* to her—didn't know what would work.

"Hey, want to hang out some time?" she asked.

"I've, uh, actually got a girlfriend. Long distance."

Under a streetlight, Lisa lifted my hand and wrote her number on the back. "In case you change your mind," she said. Then she turned and walked off, her weight swinging deliberately from one hip to the other.

I navigated the pitch black of the path, using the dim light from the garden to guide me forward. Someone was studying *The Three Shades*, the closest sculpture to the road, but disappeared into the garden.

It felt good to be back with the statues. After I flopped down on the bench I'd used before, I pulled a cigarette from one of my pockets, struck a match, and inhaled. I let the smoke out slowly through my nose. I had to have some outlet, some escape hatch for what was always boiling inside me. At least I wasn't snorting anything. I laughed to myself, thinking of all the things I could be smoking, snorting, or shooting up.

I leaned down and peered under the bench, searching for my paper from the first day of class. Nothing. The clean-up crew must have found it. It didn't matter anyway. I dug my fingers into the muscle on my thigh that sometimes acted up from a baseball injury.

When I looked up, a girl was staring at me. A girl dressed in multiple layers, yet not in the usual way. She was small, but her body looked strong. Her long hair, her eyes . . . .

"Hey," I said, almost involuntarily. "You're . . . ." It had to be her, but she was dressed so differently. No sign of my shirt.

"Hello," she said. She brushed her long bangs aside and moved next to *Caryatid with Stone*.

"I've seen you here before. Haven't I?" I asked. "You're the girl from the other night." I was absolutely sure now. She had a different quality from anyone I'd met before. It wasn't just because she was European. She had a mystery about her. I'd never been able to conjure up any scenario that would explain the night I met her.

She looked wary, or surprised to see me. I couldn't tell which.

"Hey, don't worry," I said. "I'm not stalking you or anything. Didn't mean to give you the wrong impression."

I leaned back on the bench to give her some space.

"Stalking? What does this mean?" She stepped away from the statue to confront me, her shyness gone.

"I mean, I'm not following you." She had me off balance, backpedaling.

"Well, I hope you are not." She crossed her arms.

"Listen." I softened my voice. "What was going on last night? I mean, maybe you don't want to say . . . you seem fine now, but I was worried. You were really . . . ."

"That night was my first in this garden. I was *désorientée*."

"Disoriented? You seemed like you were pretty messed up." Couldn't take it back. Damn. "That didn't come out right."

"What are you saying?"

"I'm sorry. Look, I don't mean to pry. Everyone's entitled to a bad night every once in a while."

"Yes. I think it is so." Her head was cocked to one side. I wasn't sure she knew exactly what I meant. But the edges of her mouth lifted into a smile, just for a second. Reaching under a bench, she pulled out my black shirt. "This is yours. It was very kind of you."

"Hey, thanks. Let's start over, okay? I've deleted the other night from my memory." Needed to keep her talking to me. "Are you an art student? I like your accent." I flicked off the ash that had built up on my cigarette.

"*Oui*, I am a student of art. The art of Rodin, in particular." She straightened her posture.

"So we've got something in common." That was better.

On her shoulder, what was it? "Wait a minute, stand still. Don't move," I said.

I walked toward her, my eyes focused. She was about to back away when I reached out and brushed her neck with my fingers. "A spider." Mindful of its fragile legs, I cradled it in my hand and set it on the ground.

She shivered at the sight of it. "Thank you."

I leaned against the pedestal of the caryatid statue, so close to her that I could see her eyelashes, the small creases in her lips.

"So you truly do study Rodin," she said.

"I'm doing an assignment for a night class here at Stanford." I couldn't help observing her clothes more carefully. It was definitely the layered thing, but she did it a little more haphazardly.

"What type of class?" she asked.

"Performance art. First acting class I've taken in college. First class, period."

"Performance art? What will you do for your assignment?"

"Wish I knew," I said. "I'm just exploring right now. Maybe something to do with these sculptures."

She wandered to the other caryatid statue, her arms clasped behind her back, and I followed.

"I considered the painter Jackson Pollock," I said. "But, you know, I keep coming back to Rodin. He honestly seemed like a hell of a bore when I first started researching him. But he's getting meatier, deeper, the more I get into it."

"Rodin was insecure," she said firmly. "He suffered of depression. Do not insult him."

Her tone surprised both of us.

"So you know a lot about him?"

"It is one thing I know." She tilted up her chin.

I leaned toward her. She had an innocence, yet such a confidence about her—she easily took me off guard.

"I'd love to talk to you some more," I said. "I'm trying to get beyond the surface, really investigate what kept Rodin going, where his ideas came from. You want to get some coffee? We could go downtown, or someplace on campus." I snuffed out my cigarette with my shoe and tossed the butt into the garbage.

"That does not seem to be a good idea . . . no," she said, but I could tell that she was fighting the urge to go. "Besides, I have things to do." She headed toward *The Gates of Hell.*

Yeah, right. Not what I wanted to hear, but she didn't seem to be totally brushing me off.

"Sure, okay," I said. I rubbed at my jaw trying to think of a way to postpone leaving. "Wait. What's your name?"

She hesitated for quite a while. A woman walked by holding a gray cat on a leash.

"Cat," she said as if just remembering her own name.

The sharp staccato sounds began the next day at midmorning and never stopped. It was impossible to gauge where they were coming from, and as the day progressed, they increased, sounding more and more like gunshots. I had to resist an impulse to duck beneath a picnic table. None of the many people passing through the garden seemed disturbed. Definitely, it was not wartime.

When a long-haired young man strolled into the garden arm in arm with his girlfriend in a tan beret, it created a nice distraction for me. He stopped in front of *The Gates of Hell* and pointed a silver object at *The Thinker*.

"You're way too in your head, man. Get into your body. Show me what you know."

"You're so bad, Joel." His girlfriend grinned at him, showing off the gap in her teeth.

Joel stood in front of *The Three Shades*. "Move, move. Love the camera. Love me."

I stared at the tiny boxy object he called a camera. Moving beside him, I couldn't help but ask, "What camera is that?"

"Just my Canon." When he held it up, the photograph of *The Three Shades* appeared in a window.

"Oh. A picture."

"Yep." He pointed the camera toward me, clicked a button on it, and handed it to me.

I stared at the image of my face. "Is this me?" My face was very smooth. My almond-shaped eyes and pronounced nose, they were similar to before. My nose never did fit my face. And my hair—it was wild, all over my face, streaming down my shoulders, unruly.

When the young man held out his hand, I pulled my concentration away from the picture and returned the camera. His girlfriend grabbed his arm from the other side.

"Want to get something to eat?" she asked.

"Just a sec, one more shot." He moved beside *Martyr*. "Don't be such a victim," he said, clicking the camera again.

I laughed out loud, and they turned in unison to look at me.

When the gunshots detonated loudly a few seconds later, I flinched but the two of them did not respond.

"Let's eat, Joel. I'm starving."

I was starving, too.

"Should we ask her along?" Joel whispered with enough volume for me to hear. I almost hoped she would agree.

"No." The girlfriend spoke into Joel's ear. "We're not asking Ms. Beautiful-Strange-Girl along."

When they turned their backs and strolled away, I felt even more alone, like a statue abandoned in the unkempt yard of an art studio. I wished I could sit with them, and eat and drink and laugh. I even wished I had gone with the young man when he had invited me to drink coffee with him.

But I knew that I had never been good with such social gatherings. A memory-image filled me: The feel of a wine glass against my lips, the titter of laughter and clever conversation among the people in the group. Me, impatient and fidgeting. Beside Rodin.

I drank in the image for a few minutes and then shook it off, trying to reorient myself to the garden.

By the time the sky turned dark gray, I had grown accustomed to the staccato sounds, and to my surprise the garbage cans were overflowing from all the visitors. I ate the remains of a salad with dressing along with some cold pasta, and retrieved a small cloth bag that someone had tossed into the garbage. As I was brushing a few crumbs from the outside of the violet bag, the sky seemed to explode with colored bursts of light.

Fireworks. So that was it! I had seen them before at the Eiffel Tower. On the fourteenth of July. Perhaps it was the holiday.

I sprawled on the grass behind the benches and let the sounds and shapes fill me with color. Radiant reds, blues, yellows, greens. When the display ended and I could hear only an occasional popping sound in the distance, I tugged my cotton sweater around me and crawled under the juniper.

A scratching and a rattling woke me. My muscles tensed as I peered out at the cans near my bed. I gasped. Two eyes in a black mask stared back at me. Through the darkness, I made out ears, hand-like paws, and a thick, furry body. The animal reaching into the garbage stopped his search, hopped down, and trundled off into the dark.

"Scat. That is my food," I said, laughing to myself.

———— ◆ ————

The following morning, I found a copper coin near the bronze gates. I recognized the bust of President Lincoln. The portrait was well done. I placed the coin in my small cloth bag, which at that moment became my bag of treasures. Only a half of an hour later, I noticed the silver arc of a ring poking out from the gravel. I removed my blue sock, slipped the ring on my middle toe, and admired my one piece of jewelry.

Buoyed by my finds, I explored the row of bicycles next to the garden. Each was tethered to a metal structure with a locking device. But one bicycle was loose. I knew I should not take it, but I needed a way to leave the garden, to escape when I needed to—if the garden permitted me. I wanted to see what was out there. When I was ready. Soon.

I walked the bicycle across the narrow road next to the garden and laid it on the ground beside a prickly bush surrounded by tall grass. Piles of mulch and dried grass lay in heaps about the field, so I used them to cover the bicycle. When I finished, my nails were stained a sienna brown.

———— ◆ ————

That night, after a wilted salad, *spritz, foosh,* water began to spurt like tiny fountains in the stretch of grass in front of the stone museum behind *The Gates.* Because it was the blackest part of the night, it seemed safe to strip off my clothes and stand in the cold water. Bathing refreshed me, as I carefully washed my body with my hands, smiling to myself, despite the cold. This garden seemed to be caring for me.

Afterward I huddled in my sweater, rubbed myself, and dried slowly in the cool air, annoyed that I could not shake off water like a dog or repel it like a Mandarin duck. As I braided my wet hair in the dark, a bit of the ache from my past life climbed up to the surface and almost took my breath away. I shrunk back from it, sensing that at its core was a darkness as black as India ink. What could it be inside me that was hiding so deep?

For the first time, I curled up to sleep on my bench, in order to gather strands of hope from the light pouring from the moon.

———— ◆ ————

I slept soundly, and the next day was particularly fruitful. I watched a young child race behind *The Gates of Hell* and down a ramp surrounded by cement walls.

"Stop it, Tania, you're wasting water. Turn that faucet off," her mother said, chasing after her.

Upon investigation, I found a simple drinking fountain. It was perfect for my *salle de bain*. The walls created a more private bathing room.

That evening, I carried a precious ham-filled croissant scavenged from the garbage to the steps of the outdoor restaurant that overlooked the garden, behind a row of tall thin trees. It was closed most nights. I ate my dinner eagerly next to the sculpture called *Prayer*. Out of the edge of my eye, I noticed something green tucked behind one of the tables. As I approached, I realized it was a rolled-up tablecloth. A blanket! I would be warm at night.

Back in the main garden, I tucked the blanket under my bench. When the moonlight made the bronze statues look like black stone, I was drawn to *Martyr*, and ran my hand over the features on the statue's tortured face. I did not wish to be a martyr.

But this darkness inside me . . . how could I possibly know how to repair it?

I pulled on my work shirt in the break room and buttoned it up. Doris was sitting by the card table reading a movie magazine. The morning light from the window made her cigarette smoke look like a storm cloud. A pink box of donuts sat on the table. I was pretty sure it was Jim climbing up the stairs—sounded like his boots.

"What's with our Giants?" Doris asked Jim, when he came into view. Her scratchy voice made me think she must have smoked for at least forty years. She threw down a magazine with Britney on the cover and headed for the stairs.

"They'll rally. No worries," Jim said. "Hey, Jesse. Haven't seen you in a couple days. Thought you tossed in the towel."

"Yeah, I wish."

We both pulled on our nifty navy blue aprons and checked out the assignment board.

"Shit, Nate's out. I've got produce prep," I said. "And his fucking graveyard shift."

"With Terry on board the whole time. You're screwed. I've got date check. Speakin' a dates, how's your brainy chick, Rachel?"

I tied my apron tightly around me. "It's been over a week since she called, and her texts and messages are getting shorter. It's really got me fucked up."

"Thought you were serious." Jim finished wolfing down a turkey sandwich as the clock ticked toward noon. We headed down the wooden steps, him wiping mayo off his scraggly mustache.

"So did I. But I think she hooked up with some prick at Columbia. Calls him a friend. Friend, my ass."

"Long distance."

"Yeah, what the hell am I gonna do from three thousand miles away?" I banged the wall with my fist. Dust flew from the wall, and my hand left a dent. Shit. I massaged my knuckles as we took the stairs double-time.

"Ladies, get to work." It was Terry, peering up the steps. He rubbed his hands over his almost-bald head. We both shut up and marched to our stations.

When I shouldered my way through the black rubber doors into the semi-dark of the produce room, two beat-up boxes of lettuce were waiting for me. I grabbed a head, yanked off the rotten leaves on the outside, and let the garbage fall around my feet. One down, forty-seven to go. It was going to be a long day before I got to class, and the garden.

———— ◆ ————

Marc Stein shook each of our hands and looked us straight in the eye as we entered. He had a strong grip and his stare penetrated. It was impossible to tell where he was coming from.

"Don't get too comfortable. We're doing *covers* today. Everybody's got one. Everybody thinks no one can see theirs."

"Jesse, we'll start with you. Get up here and tell us something about you."

Fuck. Why'd he have to start with me? Chip on my shoulder? Belligerent look on my face? What the hell?

I stood in front of everyone with my hands hanging down, my shoulders back. "I'm moving to Los Angeles to go to college. I'd like to be an actor . . . a director, someday."

"Who had an influence on you? On your life?"

Shit. I hunted around in my mind. "Well, my drama teacher, Ms. Mendes. She made me feel as if I could actually make it as an actor. Pushed me, gave me parts I didn't expect. Taught us practical things about the business, too."

"Thank you, Jesse. You can sit down. Now I'd like this half of the class to stand up." They gathered in the middle of the room. "You're Jesse, the way he wants you to see him."

Fuck this guy. I couldn't believe it. Everyone struck poses that were pretty macho-casual, shoulders back, head cocked. Some had half-smiles, sneers, smirks. I wanted to punch someone. Marc Stein for starters.

"Now show Jesse without his cover. When he's alone. When he's real. Jesse, this obviously isn't amateur hour. You can just observe. Stop judging."

At first, no one moved. Then a girl pulled over a chair and sat with her face in her hands. Tito started pounding on the wall. Others looked sad. How did they know? It was unreal.

"Jesse, I want to see your insides in this class and in your project. We can see through you anyway. Let go of your fear. You hear me? It's imperative. Okay, Nanette, your turn."

It was almost impossible to recover and move on. I couldn't really slip on my cover to hide behind. But it was a hell of a relief to see everyone else's attention moving on to Nanette. It was much easier to see other people's covers and insides. Lisa looked like she was ready to bolt when people acted out her insecurities.

"Good work, everyone," Marc Stein said. "Of course, you're going to drape yourself in a cover in the outside world. But this week, try not to put it on so thickly and see what happens. In performance art, we're often stripping away even more than the cover."

By the time I left class, I was pretty churned up. Everybody was. Some people stuck around outside the building, laughing and talking it out in loud voices. I headed toward the garden.

Cover. Yeah, I need a cover. I need armor at home, for Christ's sake. He'd pulverize me. As it is, I already feel strangled by the bullshit with him. Literally. Like I'm not going to fucking cover. My head throbbed. Why's it so impossible to stand up to him? Makes no fucking sense.

The whole exercise was a setup for trouble. As soon as I stopped thinking about him, my mind bounced to Rachel and the poem she'd sent me. *Removed/ Revealed/ It could just end/ Two messy teens/ Quickly dressed jeans* . . . I didn't know if she was talking about me and her, or someone else. I sure as hell didn't think of myself as a teen anymore. What was going on with her? Didn't she even care about me?

I stopped on the cement road before entering the garden, inhaled, exhaled, and slipped on my cover. It was too damn painful without it.

The crunch of the gravel was reassuring somehow. I could see her sitting on a bench. Her hair was unmistakable, even from the back.

"Hey, Cat," I said.

She didn't seem to hear me. It was almost as if she didn't recognize her name.

Then she turned my way. "Hello." She pulled at her jean skirt and adjusted her top. Color came to her neck and cheeks as she stood up. "Why do you come back here so soon?"

It was such a funny thing to say, as if she owned the sculpture garden. "I'm not allowed?" I laughed. "I've got to be invited?"

"Well, no, I suppose."

"Good." Just seeing her, I couldn't help but smile. Don't be pushy this time, I warned myself. "I've got to spend some solid time on my research for my performance. I decided on Rodin, for sure—"

"He makes a good subject."

"—after talking to you."

"Is this true?" She held onto the caryatid statue's foot.

"I wanted something I could really commit to. This class counts for college credit at the place I'm going in the fall."

"You attend university?" She sat on the edge of the pedestal.

"In Los Angeles, in a couple months. Got into Chapman. If I want to be an actor, a director, I've got to stay focused." I set my pack on the bench and lit up a cigarette.

"This profession takes much work, no?"

"For sure," I said. "I know, you're probably thinking *long shot*, but I'm obsessed . . . it's going to happen." The rest I could only mumble. "Hope like hell it does."

"I do not know this Chapman," she said.

"It's up and coming. In Los Angeles."

"Los Angeles? Is this near?"

"What?" She was so wise in some areas, and then came out with questions from left field.

"Well? Is it?"

"What do you mean?" I looked at her. "Oh, I guess you haven't been here long. It's six hours away." I drew on the cigarette, then stubbed it out. "Got to quit this shit."

"Six hours, hmmm."

"What about you, Cat?" I sat on the bench and gave her my full attention. "I never see you with any books." I loved to watch the expressions that animated her face. They were subtle and so unpredictable. She seemed to be going through a series of emotions just to answer my question.

"Oh."

A strange answer. But I let her off the hook. I patted the bench beside me, and she sat down at the other end of it.

"You can read all the books you wish," she said. "But everything you are needing to know, the statues tell to you."

"Ha! Tell that to my professor. I love that idea, though."

"You really must take the time to be with the sculptures, or you will never understand them."

"You'll have to show me what you mean."

I reached out and brushed my hand against her arm. Energy emanated from her and traveled to me. We gazed at each other for a few seconds. She seemed to be holding her breath.

"I guess I'd better get to work," I said, breaking the silence. "Unfortunately, my prof doesn't agree with you, and I've got this paper."

"You have very much to learn about Rodin," she teased.

"You're right there." I laughed. "But actually, my paper's more like a record of how I find the topic for my performance piece. If I ever do." I wrestled my laptop out of my backpack and slapped my face lightly to wake up my brain. "Don't mean to be rude, but . . . ."

"You are quite rude, *impoli*, but I am somehow getting used to it."

"Ha!" She was a trip, didn't even try to filter what she was saying.

Once I'd popped open the laptop, she couldn't stop staring at it, even stood behind me to study the screen.

"You really shouldn't read my stuff." I arched back to see her. "Just me fishing around for some topic. Me talking to myself. Some personal stuff, too."

"I do not mean to stalk your writing."

I chuckled, and she laughed with me.

When she settled on a bench near mine, she looked as comfortable as a chicken on its roost. Then she closed her eyes, and I think she was meditating. I typed up some thoughts in my running journal for class.

July 8
Jesse Lucas
Research/Topic exploration for performance piece

Rodin's a very cool guy now that I found some websites and got rid of the textbooks that made him sound like some wannabe-artist on Facebook. Although his friends might have been Victor Hugo, Manet, and Ibsen. Not bad. Actually, the deviantArt site is a better fit for him—he was the Tarantino of his time.

To see how revolutionary he was, he's got to be put into context, like everyone else.

If you watch the Mt. Rushmore special effects in *North by Northwest*, they're so primitive, but then you realize the seeds of the Bond movies are all there. Who's that artist who displayed a urinal as sculpture? That wouldn't fuck with people's heads now like it did back then. Or Pollock's drip paintings. They've become so clichéd there are books about monkeys dripping paint. Or is it cats?

Sculpting figures can be conservative these days, but back when classic art reigned, controversy was Rodin's middle name. His poses were completely unconventional, and he sculpted emotions vs. lofty subjects. I'm starting to understand him better just by spending time in the garden. Even tonight, sitting next to *Orpheus*, the energy almost knocked me over. I think the whiney quality in Rodin's letters that annoyed me so much may just have been his desperate need to be an artist, which I can relate to.

A thought: In Sam Mendes's *Road to Perdition*, lots of the medium shots look like paintings. If I film Rodin's sculptures, I could go for that effect. Or maybe off-center close-ups. But I've got to remember that it's not the filming that's the performance piece. It's the performance itself.

I closed my laptop and ran my hands though my hair. "Hey, Cat. I see what you mean about Rodin deserving some respect."

"I hope so. *Certainement*," she said.

"Maybe he's not as conservative as I thought."

"Conservative?" Her voice rose. "He changed everything. He changed all of sculpture."

"Whoa. Pretty passionate about it, huh? Don't worry. I'm starting to understand. His work holds up. Seems different, off balance. Even now." I glanced at my watch. "Damn, I've got to get going. They gave me the night shift." I quickly jammed everything into my backpack, then lingered. But Terry really came down on us if we weren't on time. And I couldn't lose my job. "I'd like to see you again, Cat. Any chance I could have your number?" I held the face of my watch between my fingers. "Damn, I really have to run."

I smiled and shrugged at her as I left. When I looked over my shoulder from way down the road, there she was, still watching me.

The next morning, before I opened my eyes, which were puffy from the night air, I could still hear his voice asking for a number. But I did not understand what this number was. I could see him in my mind's eye retreating into the darkness. I had wanted my thoughts to bind around him like strings and pull him back. This young man who appeared and disappeared, did he have something to tell me? To give me? I did not want to miss it if he did.

I opened my eyes and studied the shapes of a spider web that had been sculpted on my bench overnight. The spider was a tiny creature, only a millimeter in length. I carefully brushed off the web with my hand, keeping my eye on the spider, so he wouldn't surprise me later in the day inside my clothing. At least one such creature appeared each morning except when the spiders stayed in hiding after the garden cleaners sponged and sprayed the statues and benches. The webs set off a faint memory from my past, but the sun usually wiped it from my mind.

Midday, a guard with thinning hair marched diagonally through the garden, his badge swinging on his chest. I had seen him before, but this time he did not disappear into the museum. His black boots stopped inches from my shoes.

"Well, there, miss," he said in a voice with sharp edges. "Seen you here quite a few times."

My heart lurched. I could not think of words to say, except harsh ones. I knew that would not help me.

"Uh, *pardon, monsieur.*"

He waited.

"I appreciate the statues. I study them. In Paris, this was not of concern."

"Just checking. That's what we're here for." The guard's eyes traveled from the top of my head down to my toe ring. I wanted to push him away from me, but I sat without speaking, twisting my face into a polite smile.

From the tone of his voice, I knew I must be cautious when the guards came through several times each day. I must hide by the trees, or head to the field, or walk to the other side of the museum.

That afternoon, I decided to finally climb the massive stone steps of the museum and explore. When I peered inside, the image of my body in the glass door made me draw back and then step closer. My clothes made me look like a vagabond. I moved to the right to block out the sun for a sharper image. It was strange—the shape of my body was very like it had been in my last life. Long legs, small waist, not so tall.

My gaze shifted to inside the doors, where I could see a woman behind a desk and the skeleton of a horse carved from wood.

"Excuse me." A man in a green cap pushed open the heavy glass doors and entered the lobby. I caught a glimpse of the marble floors and grand staircases. And then of a guard in uniform. Later. Not now. Back to the benches.

When the dark summer sky enveloped the garden that night, I thought I heard a statue breathing. But it was someone entering the garden. It was him. He had returned. I grew still and observed him, half-hidden by *Orpheus*.

He slid his body onto what I now called *his bench*, his muscular legs bent and spread apart. Looking up, he saw me, and his eyes grew wider. "Cat. You're here again—you've really got a thing for this place, don't you? I thought I might lose touch with you."

He was asking questions again with words that I did not completely understand. I could not permit him to ask all the questions.

"What is your name?" I asked.

"Never did tell you, did I? It's Jesse."

"Jesse. This surprises me. It can be a girl's name, no?"

"Kind of blunt, aren't you?" He shook his head and chuckled.

"Am I? Comparing to what? To you?"

"Okay, forget it. You win." He raised his arms in surrender. He seemed to be trying to get me to laugh. And he did.

"What will you write about today?" I asked. "Will you do research that is more serious?"

"Well, ye-ah. Are you saying I'm not the best researcher?" He smiled, making the lines around his mouth distinct and deep. "I'm reading about Rodin's early sculptures, like *The Vanquished*, and starting in on Camille Claudel, his muse."

I pressed my hand on my chest bone to steady myself. "Camille Claudel?"

"I don't know enough about her yet," he said. "Thought I might get to that today if I have time. I read that she came to some miserable end, and it kind of depressed me. So I put it off."

Miserable end? I tried to push down a wave of anxiety. "It depressed *you*?" There was an edge to my voice that I did not expect.

"Yeah, I get depressed sometimes," he mumbled. "Doesn't every-body? Not sure why I'm telling you." His eyes narrowed, and he seemed to be picturing something disturbing. "Never mind."

I could not leave it be. "How is it that you can be depressed?" I gripped the arm of his bench and leaned toward him. "You must have a bed, a home. A mother. A father."

He curled one fist into a ball and wrapped his other hand tightly around it, as if to hide it. Then he slowly uncurled his hands and his entire body drooped. "Yeah. I've got a mother . . . a father. Sometimes that's not enough."

His posture made me sorry for my attack. I found a space to sit on the low pedestal of *Caryatid with Urn*, where I contemplated what he had said, trying to picture my own mother's face. Only an unclear image appeared. But I felt a tightening in my stomach and the chill of a cold wind.

"I see that can be true sometimes," I said. "Will you tell to me about your family?"

"Let's leave it alone, okay?" His voice was almost a growl, and his eye twitched.

I observed him further. The curve of his cheek, the lines under his eyes, the furrow between his brows that could have been made by a trowel in clay. The muscle in his jaw, his fist clenching in his right hand like the pumping of a heart. He seemed to have a well of dark feelings inside him.

We both knew a darkness. I was certain of it.

"I am sorry, Jesse. I think I understand what it is you were meaning to say."

"Forget it. Don't worry about it," he said without looking up. He pulled out his typewriter, and began to write.

A few minutes later, female voices to my right pulled me in. A mother and daughter who looked very much alike settled themselves at one of the picnic tables and began talking in low voices that rose as the conversation progressed. I moved to my bench and listened.

"I need more freedom." The daughter's eyes were downcast.

"But how can I trust you, sneaking out at two A.M.?" The mother kneaded her forehead.

"I'm only doing that 'cause you've got me on a short leash."

The mother stretched her hand toward her daughter's, but the girl clasped her hands between crossed legs.

"I'm just worried for your safety, honey."

"If you trusted me, things'd be better."

"Okay, then. What do you think is reasonable?"

"A one o'clock curfew."

"Well, maybe. But, honestly . . . are you drinking?"

They rose and wandered out of the garden together.

I knew I never had such a mother, and an image appeared in my mind: the lace at a woman's throat, dark hair pulled back tightly from her face, the scowl on her lips as she looked at me. My mother.

I cringed and pinched at the flesh on my forearm. To distract myself, I walked to the stone plaque in front of the garden. I had scanned it quickly before, but now I concentrated on each line. *Rodin 1840–1917.* The newspaper heading had read 2008. I calculated in my head. He had died ninety-one years ago.

New memory-images surfaced: Rodin surrounded by preliminary plaster figures for *The Gates of Hell*, his beard and oversize smock spackled with white, his hands chipping at the arm of a tortured man on all fours, *Ugolino*.

Shaken, I glanced at Jesse, wanting to make sense of all these dates, these images. When he remained focused on his typewriter, I allowed myself to be soothed by the soft *pum pum* of his fingers, though this was new for me: any sense of comfort.

I had to admit to myself that it was soothing when he was here, this young man who seemed so *compliqué*, so complicated. Whom I was just beginning to know.

*S*o much about Rodin's life was surprising to me. I was more and more certain something would surface to base my project on. It was a drag to write it all down, but Marc Stein was right. The journal was helping me formulate an idea.

July 10
Jesse Lucas
Research/Topic exploration for performance piece

Rodin's sculpture, *The Vanquished*, made it into the Paris Salon—that was a big deal. But his work was put down for the most fucked-up reason: It looked so real, they thought he'd created a mold by slapping plaster around a live model.

Rodin wrote pitiful letters he shouldn't have sent, circulated photos of himself with the model. Mistake. When he finally sucked it up and stopped trying to defend himself, he started sculpting larger than life. Great solution. Reminds me of Woody Allen. Even though people were on his case for dropping straight comedy, he just kept making one movie per year, and now he's got *Vicky Cristina Barcelona*, a real gem.

But Rodin couldn't win for losing. They were all over him because he didn't sculpt historically-significant-boring events, because he didn't smooth out his figures, because he used distorted body proportions. An Iggy Pop song says something about how unbearable it is when things are too normal. Maybe Rodin felt that way, too, because his stuff's not slick and polished. Sometimes that Iggy lyric keeps me from hyperventilating.

Idea for filming: Maybe I could alter the sculptures in a nonpermanent way to exaggerate the emotions on the faces, or maybe they don't need it. I'm still thinking about what the prof said about the camera seeing through your skin. Could it see through the skin of the statues?

Question: When did Rodin meet Camille Claudel and how? All I know is she came from a proper family and they met when she was young. Her brother was a well-known poet. She was a sculpture student? Her sister was a musician? In photos, her mother looks like the epitome of severe, and her father resembles a leprechaun. I think Camille was Rodin's model—isn't that how it worked in those days?

I clicked my laptop shut, rolled my shoulders, and massaged the tension from my face.

"Rodin died ninety-one years ago," Cat said out of nowhere.

"When you put it like that, he seems ancient." I straightened my legs one by one and stretched them. "I'm usually into contemporary artists, like this guy Nauman I just discovered. He does neon sign art, performance art. You know him?"

"I do not know this man Nauman," she said, "but with some artists, like Rodin, age is not important."

"Riight. It's too late to switch anyway. I signed up for Rodin, and I've already started researching the guy, so . . . ."

"Guy? What do you mean? He is a master." She pushed at my outstretched leg. "You are *impudent*. That is what you are."

"Sor-ry." I tried to disguise my laugh as a cough. "You'll be glad to know I'm starting to have a visceral reaction to Rodin's sculptures."

"If you were his apprentice, showing respect would be required."

"Where did that come from? I feel like we're in the movie *Memento* and I haven't looked at my latest tattoo yet."

"*Impudent* and *incomprehensible*," she said, trying to stay serious, but not succeeding.

"I've been called worse things," I said, grinning at her. "But, honestly, if I'd been his apprentice, I would have been fired day one. I know something about acting, but I'm just into art. No talent there."

"Into art?"

"I just like it, it resonates with me. I even have a collection of ceramic pieces—discards this sculptor-friend gave me." I rubbed my eyes, wished I didn't have to go. "Cat, listen, I really want to talk more about Rodin. Seriously. But I think it'll have to be tomorrow night? I'm beat." I sighed before I even knew it was coming. "I'd like to find out more about you, too, Cat . . . if you'll let me."

"Tomorrow night," she said.

"I promise I'll be here. Less exhausted, hopefully."

We stared at each other with an intensity that made it hard to pull away. After I left, I remembered her eyes. I wondered if she was looking forward to tomorrow as much as I was.

———◆———

Next day at the grocery store, Jim called up at me from the bottom of the break room stairs, "We're both out back for the morning. Bring your shades."

"Cool. I'll be there in a minute."

When I peeked into the break room, Doris was sitting at the card table with Olivia, the new girl, flipping through magazines. I knew they didn't see me because Doris said, "I'd let him do me for one night."

"He's not my type," Olivia said, "but this guy . . . ."

When I came into view, Olivia set down her magazine and avoided my eyes. But not Doris.

"Knock next time, Jesse. Don't you have any manners?" she teased.

"Don't let me stop you," I laughed. "Go ahead. I'm leaving."

I bounded down the stairs, still chuckling, pushed through the rubber doors, and made my way to the back of the store.

Jim had already started breaking down the boxes. "Damn, I just cut myself on a fucking staple. I'm not getting paid enough for this," he laughed.

"We have to break down this whole pile?"

"Yeah, but who cares. We're out from under Terry's eye and we got assigned together. Hey, Jess, did you see that good-looking chick in the short shorts walking through produce?"

"Nope. But you sound interested."

"She was a little old for me, but fun to watch . . . forgot you've got a girlfriend. Or do you, bud?"

I stomped on a cardboard box and flattened it. "Things are fucked. Rachel sent a cryptic poem. The more I think about it, the more I think it's her way of dumping me. But I'm not even sure. It couldn't be much worse."

"Ouch. Women can be brutal."

"For sure," I said, then muttered, mostly to myself, "I can't believe I'm even thinking about this other girl."

"Nooo," Jim said, slapping a flattened box onto the growing pile. "Can't leave any chicks for the rest of us, huh? Course, your taste. Jesus."

"Well, you have no taste at all. Your only requirement is heels. I've seen you following women down the aisles, asking if they need help. You've got no pride."

"So what's your requirement? Must-fuck-you-over?"

"Shut the fuck up, Jim." I wrestled with a large box. "You know, I can't really figure this girl out. She's . . . mysterious."

"You're such a goner, look at you. Where'd you meet her? In the parking lot? Your fancy class?"

"Hey, smartass, I met her in the sculpture garden at Stanford."

"Well, there you go. Who hangs out at a place like that?"

"Me, asshole. You should try it. I've been telling you since day one you should go back to school."

"Yeah, right. Me and classwork. Besides, then we'd be competing for the same chicks, and you wouldn't have a chance."

"You've got a point there," I laughed.

"Hey, by the way, keep away from Olivia."

"That new checker? No problem." I chucked Jim lightly on the arm. "Damn, being out here in the sun makes me want to make a run for it."

"Know what ya mean. Oh, shit, forgot to tell you, Terry wants you to take an extra shift."

"What the fuck? I'll miss class." And I couldn't go back to the garden to see Cat. "He's always pulling this crap on me."

———————————•◆•———————————

Sure enough, the night shift without Jim was hell—the hours passed so slowly. The only good thing was that Terry was too busy hounding the new girl to jump all over me. By the time I got home, I was dead tired.

Mom was watching *Casablanca*. She stopped in mid-stitch and smiled at me, running her hand over the blue and green quilt she was working on. She made up her own patterns. This one looked like a variation on the pinwheel.

"I could watch this movie every day for the rest of my life."

"I've got to buy that DVD for you."

"Did you hear from your roommate at Chapman yet?"

"Yeah, he wrote me on Facebook. Seems pretty cool. Music major. Plays guitar and piano. He's from L.A. Greg Berger."

"That's nice. A roommate can make a big difference. Mine was so different from me. She became a physicist, and I was an English major."

"Ha."

"Show me Greg's picture sometime, if you don't mind. Your dinner's waiting in the kitchen."

"Sure, Mom. You know, if you don't have the energy, I can make my own dinner sometimes."

"Then I'd feel more useless than I already do."

"Don't talk like that. I mean it."

I heated up the homemade soup until it bubbled and took it upstairs. Then I looked over the syllabus, slopping a little soup on it, and tried to do the assignment for class—more research for the project. Found some sites I needed and printed them out, since Marc Stein wanted to see all our sources.

I flipped through a library book while the printer cranked away.

I jumped when the door swung open. I'd been so absorbed in the pictures of Rodin sculpting, I hadn't heard him on the stairs. Not smart.

"Dad, you gotta knock."

"I don't gotta do anything."

"Okay. I'm just trying to work."

"What do you know about work? If you don't get your hands dirty, it's not really work, now is it?" He smiled at me.

"There's all kinds of work, Dad."

"Think you're better than me, huh?"

"No." He was halfway across the room. I shifted in my chair so I was sitting sideways, my feet firmly on the floor, my hands free.

"You could have it all with sports, Jesse. That's where the money is. Think about where you could be in four years, son." He looked out the window. "You have no idea how much I looked forward to sitting at your games. I would have driven to any college to watch you play."

"I know, Dad. I just don't want it that much."

"That school you're going to doesn't even have a football team, does it?" His voice was too calm.

"No."

"Or a baseball team."

"No."

"That's all you can say? *No?* Thought you were so smart. Weren't even smart enough to pick a college with sports teams."

He was almost to my chair. His neck was red. Fuck.

Before I could get out of the way, he knuckled me in the upper arm, hard, two times. I jumped up, holding my arm, then took a defensive fighting pose. Dad laughed and teased me with fake jabs, a light slap at my face, and then punches at my stomach. I fended off one punch, swung at his face. Missed. His next punch landed on my ribs. I sucked in my breath with the pain, and put up my arms again. He lowered his hands and swaggered out of the room.

I gritted my teeth and tried not to take as many breaths. "Fucking asshole. Fuckin' asshole."

I popped some ibuprofen I had on my desk and downed some old water in a thermos from my shelf. Had to be some form of PTSD or something, from all the beating he took from his dad. Looked it up once, and it mostly fucking fit—shit, maybe I had it, too. Or maybe he was just your garden-variety alcoholic.

When the seething inside me subsided to a semi-functional level, I willed myself to get back to my books. Diving into Rodin's life calmed me down a little. I flipped through photos of *The Gates of Hell*, which was commissioned really early on. So many powerful sculptures in one giant piece.

About an hour later, when I heard footsteps on the stairs, I leapt up, jarring my ribcage. Grabbed my baseball bat and waited behind the door, trying to even out my breathing.

"You fucker," I whispered. "I will cave in your fucking skull, crack it open, and leave you for dead."

He was approaching. Coming down the hallway. I gripped the bat tighter.

Then, suddenly, my muscles went limp and I shoved the bat under my bed, just before Dad fell against the outside of the door.

He staggered in, hanging onto the bookshelf to steady himself. I could smell his breath from a couple feet away. "How ya doing, Jesse? I just figure you gotta toughen up, ya know."

I walked backwards.

"My pop toughened me up." He followed me and pretended to punch me in the arm.

I tried not to wince, as he held my shoulder and squeezed. "I'm prouda you, son. I just hate to see you throwin' away your future, that's all. You know that, don't ya?"

I nodded, hoping my eyes didn't give me away.

When *tomorrow night* finally arrived, I waited on my bench, glancing up whenever someone stepped onto the gravel. But the night grew dark as a crow's wing, and I felt my spirit weakening and my insides flaring in anger at him. Jesse never appeared.

"I must forget him," I muttered. I fumbled for my blanket and threw it onto the bench. A groan of impatience came from my throat. I could not wait for someone so careless with his promises. He did not have the answers for me. Whatever I was needing, it was outside the garden.

The next morning, I heaved the bicycle out from under the mulch, brushed off the dirt, and straddled the seat. If the garden did not stop me from leaving, I was ready to explore. Pedaling down the cement road felt like leaving home for the first time. When I glanced back, the garden seemed to bid me, "*Bonne chance*, good luck."

Within minutes, a large vista opened below me, an oval of deep green grass with patches of wildflowers. Some young people were throwing a flat disc among themselves. Others were lying about, reading or napping. Through an archway at the top of the oval, I could see stone buildings and a large church, its face covered with colored tiles.

"Oh," I said out loud. There was so much to see. I should have left the garden sooner.

After I crossed the street, a set of familiar bronze figures caught my eye. *The Burghers of Calais*! I walked my bicycle past a row of narrow arches until I was beside them. Each shackled man was lost in thought, prepared to sacrifice his life to save his town. I touched the hand of the nearest figure, triggering a memory of Rodin's studio: The burgher's hand I had modeled, still moist, was resting on a slab of wood. I was presenting it to Rodin and he was nodding approvingly.

I wheeled my bicycle back to the road and rejoined the flow of walkers and riders, mostly young men and women. With the other travelers, I rode past the front of the stone buildings and turned right onto a tree-lined path. In the distance, I picked a random point as my destination. I knew I should not wander too far, and all the while I tried to remember landmarks: a small museum, a sculpture that appeared to be the bones of a pelvis. *Henry Moore, Large Torso,* the plaque read. I had never seen such a sculpture with so much simplicity.

In the stones beside the statue, something black stood out among the gray. I bent and picked up a tiny doll's shoe made of a pliable material, with a small bow molded onto the front. As I closed my hand around it, for a moment I felt like a young girl in France again. I added it to the collection in my cloth bag before hopping back onto my bicycle.

At the spot I had planned to stop, I smelled food. The aroma was emanating from a stand with a rippled, overhanging roof, alongside which a dozen people were lined up in a row. Those who were leaving clutched paper cups with steam escaping from them. The air smelled like hot coffee. I noticed a basket of bright pink and orange fruits for sale and watched people nibbling muffins and croissants at round tables. My mouth watered.

Someone had abandoned half a brioche on a table in the shade. I casually walked by, snatched the pastry in its napkin, and squeezed it into the pocket of my sweater. Gift secured, I turned around and headed back home to the garden, using all my willpower not to eat the brioche as I pedaled.

When the sun was directly overhead, I reached the garden. I found a small block of orange-colored cheese left on the picnic table, ripped it into pieces, and savored each morsel on bits of the brioche. As I was finishing, two young women entered the garden holding hands. They sat at one of the tables, on the same side, facing out.

"Why can't you commit?" the taller girl said. They seemed not to care if I overheard them.

"Why? Because we haven't known each other that long."

"But you said you were into me." The tall girl held the other's shoulders and kissed her, passionately. It brought forward a memory-image of one of Rodin's drawings of lesbians. He was obsessed with them.

"You think you can manipulate me, don't you?" the shorter girl interrupted my memory.

"Manipulate you? I love you."

"Flows off the tongue pretty easily. I know about you and commitment."

They both stood and walked off together, their hands hanging stiffly at their sides.

As I looked carefully at *The Gates of Hell*, I reflected on the couple and tried not to think of Jesse. I could not be certain when he would return, or if he would return at all. I could not help but be furious with myself that I had looked forward to his visit, that I had expected him to come back *tomorrow*. I rubbed at the ache in my chest as a glimmer of memory surfaced. I could feel the memory traveling like a venom through my body, but I could not picture it: It was a feeling of deep disappointment that seemed to be tethered to a promise made and broken by Rodin.

*N*ext class, when I explained my absence the night before, Marc Stein was too busy fussing with his camera battery to make a big thing of it. I had a hard time covering the dark mood I was in from my encounter with Dad. Tried to be invisible in class. Thankfully, Marc Stein left me alone.

When I entered the garden, I wasn't in any better shape. I could see her sitting on a low cement seat in front of the gates, eating out of a plastic container. Looked like sushi. My sandals seemed to slog through the gravel as if it were mud.

She froze when she saw me, then glared.

"What?" I asked. My shoulders tensed.

"I cannot trust you."

"What the . . . ?"

"You do not keep to your promises."

"I don't need this." Fuck. Now *she* was on the attack.

I slumped down on a low platform near hers, eyes focused on the gravel. With my knuckles I kneaded my temples and my jawbone. My eyelid twitched. I was really fucked up.

I knew I shouldn't be there. I scooted forward to get up and leave. But just then, she sat down beside me. Her mood seemed to have shifted completely. Out of the corner of my eye, I could see her reaching out to touch my hair, then drawing her hand back.

"Go ahead." I wanted her to touch me. I wanted to feel the warmth of her fingers. Her cheeks were flushed, and she curled her hand into her lap. "It's okay. Touch me if you want."

But the moment had passed.

I leaned toward her. I had to be the one to make the move. She let me lean close enough that my lips were nearly touching hers.

Then she drew back.

"No, this is not good," she said.

"Why isn't it good?" I asked. Very confusing.

"You need commitment. Today, they said this in the garden, and I agree."

So unexpected. I almost laughed. She actually got me to stop thinking about myself and all my shit. "You sometimes talk in riddles, you know."

"Two girls kissed today in the garden. One wanted commitment."

"O-kay. They were just one couple." I rubbed the stubble on my chin, smiling at her. "Kissing is definitely allowed without commitment," I said, pulling her up from the bench. "Come on." A current seemed to flow from the soft skin of her hand to mine.

She stared at the fresh bruise on my upper arm, and I froze.

"What is this?" she asked.

"I'm an athlete. That's one of the perks." My eyelid twitched. "Takes a while to go away."

She let it go and followed me into the museum, up the metal staircase. My sandals flapped loudly on every step. Our hands, interwoven, reminded me of the beginning stitches of the embroidery my mom sometimes did. I led her into the circular room lined with Rodin's statues and stopped in front of one of my favorites.

"*The Kiss*." I made a flourishing gesture toward the sculpture. "Even though, apparently, Rodin didn't think much of this sculpture, he did approve of kissing." I smirked. I had her there.

"So you think you have so much culture," she said, without looking at the statue. "The lips of Paolo and Francesca do not touch."

How could it be? I crouched down and looked up. "Huh? Well . . . that's just an artistic choice." How did she know without checking? She must have studied it thoroughly. "But women and men do kiss without commitment."

"Perhaps in these times, only the women kiss," she said, smiling.

"Right," I laughed. "In the twenty-first century, it's only for women."

I moved close to her and placed my hand behind her head, threading my fingers through her hair. Gently, I tilted her head toward mine, my hand on the curve at the back of her neck. I wanted to feel her lips so bad.

My mouth brushed against hers.

She pushed away from me, stumbling a bit as she backed up. "You think I want to share you with someone?"

"Where are you coming from?" This was crazy.

"You have someone. A girl you are close to. It is true, no? She has very blonde hair . . . ."

"Well, I have a girlfriend. Sort of. But, no, she has red hair." Blonde? Had she seen me with Lisa?

She looked confused, then sure again. "You cannot kiss me if you are with someone else."

"Okay, listen—not that I'm condoning it . . . ." I took a step away from her. "But technically if you go back in history, even Rodin had a mistress. Camille Claudel."

"*Oui*, he did." She was almost shouting. "Next you will say we can make love without attachment." Her cheeks turned pink, and she looked as if she wished she could take back her words. But they were already floating in the gallery air between us. I inhaled. She literally took my breath away.

"Whew, you move fast," I said. Then, "Never thought I'd hear myself say something like that."

"It is time that you go." Was she kidding? Her stance said no.

"You're serious, aren't you? I hope you'll give me another chance." I didn't want to leave. She had a strange way of pulling me in and pushing me away.

"Another chance? . . . Maybe, Jesse. But you have to go now. I must have time for myself."

Her boundaries around herself seemed almost impenetrable. But I honestly thought I could get through.

"Okay, but I'll see you tomorrow?"

"If you come tomorrow." Her voice had a touch of sarcasm.

I walked out of the museum, not knowing what to think. I was helpless—not a feeling I liked. I had to do what she said, but only for now. Underneath it all, I felt as if she needed me and I needed her, no matter what she said.

I stayed behind, by *The Kiss*. I could not believe that I even thought to trust another man.

But I could still hear the timbre of his voice at its gentlest, could still smell the musk of his clothes, could still see the bit of puffiness beneath his eyes. I waited, giving him time to leave before departing myself. My feelings were tumbling, like stream water over rocks. I walked past the sculptures in the back section of the garden, behind the row of tall trees, and hesitated at each one—*Prayer, The Walking Man, Falling Man.* Rodin put so much emotion into his sculptures.

I was drawn back to *Prayer* and stroked the statue's smooth thighs. To be human, to be alive, it was so *compliqué*. It was a mystery to me how people found the courage to be truly close with another person. I shivered in the warm night air.

Is this what I must learn? I was not certain I could find the courage.

———•◆———

"Bitch. Cunt."

I was woken from a deep sleep by a low, raspy voice that sounded like the remnant of a nightmare. It was a man's voice, and it seemed to be coming from the cement road. I could hear him approaching, but his footsteps were irregular, as if he were stumbling and catching himself.

I grabbed my blanket and dashed behind the juniper. The footsteps grew louder. I needed to hide. Quickly.

"Wha' the hell she thinkin'?" He was by Jesse's bench.

More voices, but this time coming from behind me. I ducked down. I could see them, and hear them laughing. Three young men. One of their shirts displayed Greek letters, on another was the word *Stanford.*

"I am so fucked up."

"That's your default state 'a mind."

"What am I doing with you losers?"

They laughed, and one dropped a can and stomped on it.

"Let's crash at your place, Tito."

After they traipsed diagonally through the garden, I listened for the first man's low voice. The call of a night bird and the motors of automobiles sounded in the distance, but that was all. The young men had chased him away.

I slept the rest of the night underneath my juniper.

———— ◆ ————

I was relieved to see the sun. At least the days were safe. One of my tops smelled of me on a hot summer day, so I washed it in the fountain and hung it on a tree branch in the field. Then I continued my study of *The Gates of Hell.* Some of the figures seemed to lean out and beckon to me, reminding me that I had helped to cast them. I ran my fingers over the writhing bodies until I could not reach any higher, even on tiptoe.

I had to make art in some way. My fingers were impatient for it. I had to do more than wait for Jesse's visits, even if we were meant to know each other.

A soft yip. "Here, Patches. That's a good boy." A woman with muscles defined in her legs was marching toward the garden with a small black and white, curly-haired dog. The woman's outfit consisted of very short pants that barely covered her buttocks and a shirt without sleeves. She tied the dog's leash to the leg of Jesse's bench and moved to the grass where she stretched her legs at different angles.

"I'll be back, Patches." She kissed the top of the dog's head and ran off.

I approached the dog slowly, my hand outstretched, palm down. "Hello, Patches. May I touch you?"

Patches wiggled and whined and licked at my cheek. I crouched beside him and stroked his head and ears. He allowed me to put my arms around him and pat his back. Except for Jesse's hand on my hand and in my hair, I had not been touched. I sighed deeply and felt how much I needed it. But it was difficult to let myself be touched by him, though I wanted it.

It seemed strangely important that I go beyond my fears with Jesse. Yet the arms of my past seemed always to be pulling me back.

I knelt beside Patches for more than half of an hour, until I heard strong breathing behind me. Turning, I saw the woman holding her sides and bending at the waist.

"Your dog, he is beautiful," I said.

"He's such a pal, isn't he?" Then to the dog, "I can always depend on you, huh, Patches?"

I walked down the road in front of the garden, surrounded by darkness. And there was Cat. It was as if we were in a routine now. As if we'd both silently agreed that this was our meeting place.

"Hey, Cat." I slid in next to her on her bench.

She stared at my hands as I opened my pack. I could have sworn she wanted me to touch her again—even kiss her—right then.

"Are you speaking to me today, after sending me packing yesterday?" I couldn't keep my lips from creeping into a smile.

"*Oui*, Jesse. I will speak with you."

"Good," I said. "What a day it's been." I piled a few books onto the bench. "My computer's been acting up. I'm so dependent on it. Today I was supposed to send some forms back for registration at Chapman, and it kept freezing." I balanced it on top of the books.

She studied my computer intensely, as if it was a new model. Then she turned away, bent down toward the gravel by the bench, and picked up a tiny spring, like from inside a watch. Over and over, she contracted it between her fingers.

"Do you have a sheet of paper?" she asked "This spring reminds me that I need to use my hands."

"Lined paper okay?"

She nodded. "Can I borrow a pencil or a pen?"

"Sure. What for?"

"I want to sketch, instead of staring at you as you work," she said, teasing me. "I know you enjoy this, but . . . ."

"You think you know what I'm thinking, what I enjoy, huh?" I laughed and handed her a few pieces of paper, a pencil, and a book to draw on.

"*Mais oui*, I do." Immediately, she sat on her hoodie in the gravel, her back to me, and began sketching *Caryatid with Stone*. While I worked, I kept glancing over at her. She seemed to be making quick sketches of the face, hands, and feet, then the whole figure—definitely drawing with a lot of confidence.

When she held the paper at arm's length, I set my laptop on the bench and kneeled beside her. "That's incredible. You obviously understand anatomy, but it's the lines. They're so strong. They give the drawing volume, like a sculpture."

"Thank you. Although I do not need you to approve me, you know," she said, smiling.

"Damn, do I know that," I laughed. "Listen, Cat, you like to keep me guessing, but what's your story? You're from another country . . . France, right?"

She hesitated. "*Oui*, I am, I suppose."

"Cat, this isn't a game. I want to know you." I stretched out my arm self-consciously, slowly, like a bird unfolding its wing. I reached out to stroke her hair, but then I drew it back, thinking better of it. She looked disappointed, but I couldn't be sure.

"Do you live around here?" I asked, resettling myself on the bench.

"*Oui*, I do. I live here," she said.

"Are you a student? Do you go to Stanford?"

"I am a student. I learn all the time."

"Okay, so, you obviously weren't born here. Where'd you grow up?" I bent toward her, listening. I didn't want to disturb the moment, now that she was actually answering.

"It is difficult to say. I am here now . . . and have been for a long time . . . but for many years, I lived in Paris."

"I'm guessing that's how you got so interested in Rodin."

"*Oui*, we were living in the same city." She leaned back against the wrought iron arm of the bench.

"Damn, you must have spent a lot of time at the Rodin Museum there," I said, struggling to extract a large art book from my pack. "What's it like compared to this garden?"

"The Rodin Museum?"

"You didn't think I'd look that up?" I asked, squinting at her. "Did you get to see Rodin's old studio? It must be a whole different thing to study him in Paris."

"To study with him," she said, her voice muted. Her eyes were distant, as if she was picturing something from the past.

It took me a second to speak. "You're charming, you know. Poetic, really. It would be like studying with him, in a way. I read that he had lots of apprentices in his studios. All women, I think."

"*Oui.* All women."

Her back straightened. Strange.

"He seemed to have his favorites." I set my laptop on my legs.

"*Certainement,*" she said, turning away.

She seemed so uncomfortable, I decided to leave her alone. When I began writing, she smoothed out a blank paper and looked around, as if searching for a subject. I knew she was considering me. What would she see? My bad habit of clenching my jaw? The bruise near my ear? My insides? I tried not to worry about it—she looked so content, drawing me.

"Where are you from?" she asked, studying my face.

"What?"

"Your family."

"Oh. My mom's side is from Romania. My dad's family is from Norway."

"Oh, *à l'opposé.* You are a combination of opposites."

"Yeah, I guess I am."

I peeked every once in a while to check out her drawing. She'd accentuated my unruly mass of hair, the broadness of my forehead, the bones of my cheeks and chin. It almost looked like she was preparing to mold a sculpture of my head.

Drawing seemed to come so naturally to her, and she definitely didn't mind me watching her. Maybe it was the only way she knew to show me who she was. Maybe it was her way of getting closer to me.

"*H*ey, remember that girl I met?"

Jim was stamping dates on all the cans in aisle two. I straightened them on the shelves, tossed outdated stuff in a cart, and moved everything forward.

"Yeah. What's the latest?"

"Ya know, I'm still confused about her."

"What's to be confused about? She pretty?"

I nodded.

"Brainy, like you like 'em?"

"Yeah."

"So what's the problem?"

"She's skittish. So private."

"I'd drop her, then," Jim smiled with half his mouth.

"Fuck it, Jim. Seriously. If she's not an art history major, what the fuck's up with her?"

"Why do you insist on figuring chicks out? Just have a good time."

"That's your M.O., dude. Something's really got a grip on her."

"Shit. She's got you goin'. You're fucked, man."

"Thanks."

"Anytime. Hey, bro, I'm thinking of asking Terry for a boost in pay."

"Go for it. You deserve it. You been here for, what? Three, four years?"

"And all during high school. All at this same charming locale."

"Jesus. Ask for double your pay."

The day dragged on, but I used the time to think. After work, I stopped by the Art Mart around the corner. It was still full daylight when I got to the garden. First time.

She was in the field. I could have sworn I saw her lifting her hoodie off the limb of a tree. She came back toward the benches and startled when she caught sight of me.

"You are so early." She inspected me closely, as if I was a work of art.

"No class today. Prof's sick. But it's been a good day. I found out I got into this class on visual storytelling at Chapman."

"What do you learn in this class?"

"We get to write, film, and edit short pieces. And we'll be the crew for each other's films."

"This makes you happy, I see."

"Yeah, it does. Oh—"

I dug out a chocolate-brown sketchpad from my pack, brushed it off, and handed it to her. "For you . . . to make *you* happy."

She inhaled its bittersweet smell and held it to her chest. "This is so nice. The nicest thing anyone has done for me . . . in this lifetime."

"What the hell, Cat? How could that be?"

"It simply is."

I'd always veered away from discussing her clothes, but I couldn't help myself. "You seem like a minimalist. Not a lot of outfits, or stuff. Don't need a big closet. And don't have much trouble with clutter, huh?"

"*Minimaliste*? I suppose I agree. And you, you are a teaser, no? Is that the right word?"

"Pretty close. I've been called that before. So . . . I've always wondered about your socks. Any significance there?"

She looked away. A sore spot?

"How do you mean, about my socks?"

I grinned and put up my palms toward her in a defensive gesture, to lighten things up. "Hey, I like the way you look. The archetypal art student."

"Jesse, you make many conclusions, about things you know little about. In your research . . . and about me." She was standing with a hand on her hip.

"Maybe."

"You must take time."

"So you're saying I jump to conclusions?" My neck was turning red, for sure. "I wouldn't have to do that if you'd throw me a bone every once in a while." Shit, her evasiveness was making me start to think she was sleeping on people's couches. Or had absolutely no money. Or was living in a car. That would be fucked up.

"Throw a bone?" She cocked her head.

"Tell me something about you. That's what it means."

Silence.

Damn. This wasn't working.

I took her hand and led her to a picnic table near the caryatids, hopped onto it, and sat cross-legged. When I patted the table, she climbed up and sat opposite me, with her legs underneath her.

"So what were you like when you were little?" I asked. "What'd you like to do?" That seemed safe.

"Hmmm. I loved the feel of dirt, of stones, and especially clay— pounding it, shaping it with my hands. My life had worth once I found clay." Her cheeks were pink.

"So you were into art really early. Interesting. You've been doing it your whole life."

"*Oui.*"

Her distant look told me that was it for now—with the questions.

"Give me your hands," I said. "Just for fun, okay?"

I stretched my hands out in front of me, palms up, then motioned for her to put her hands on top of mine. When she did, I slapped her hands lightly.

"You are rude! Why do you do this?" she yelped.

I gently placed my hands back under hers, and slapped again.

"Ah, it is a game," she laughed. But she drew her hands back and hid them in her lap. "What did you like?" she asked.

"What do you mean?"

"When you were little."

"Oh. Baseball. I was obsessed with baseball."

"Hmm?"

"You know, you hit a ball with a bat . . . oh, maybe it's not so big in France. I was pretty damn good." I remembered back to the long afternoons when Dad pitched to me. "My dad taught me." A current of sadness passed through me, and I could feel my jaw clench. But I straightened up and tried to will myself to snap out of it. "I read a lot, too."

I took her hands in mine to play the game again. This time she was ready and pulled them away before the slap.

"Hey, you got it," I said, and we laughed at the same time. "Your turn now."

I placed her hands in the slapper's position, underneath mine. She moved her fingers slightly, making me flinch, and then slapped my hands hard.

"You hurt me," I whined, feigning an injury. It made her smile. "So what about friends? You have a lot of friends growing up?"

"My brother is the person I was close with. He was a poet." She looked me directly in the eyes. "In my family, you needed strong allies to survive."

"Sounds rough."

She sank inside herself, but amazingly, she spoke her thoughts out loud, "My father had a temper. My mother was disappointed in me." She took in a breath and let it out. "What about you, Jesse? Who was your friend?"

"We moved around a lot. My dad kept changing jobs," I said. Then, under my breath: "Was forced to change jobs." I cleared my throat. "Anyway, my first friend was Johnny. After that, wherever we were, I looked for someone whose name started with J." I grinned at her.

"Did you find anyone? I can almost imagine you as a young boy."

"Not for a while. But I was friends with a guy named Jack in high school," I chuckled, "and I had a dog named Jasper."

Our laughing overlapped again, and we leaned in toward each other. She held her neck so gracefully, I wanted to move her hair back and touch it. But instead, I carefully placed my hand under hers, squeezed it as tenderly as I could, and massaged the palm. She let me.

Then she adjusted my hands back into position for the game. When I caught her hand in a slap, she cried out in what sounded like delight.

"Gotcha," I said. "So now you know about Jasper. Did you have any pets?"

"Pets?"

"Like cats or dogs?"

"Oh, my mother did not allow it, although many people had dogs in Paris."

"You were born there?"

"No, but my family moved there because I insisted on studying art."

"Your family relocated for you?"

"*Oui*. After some time. I was quite *obstinée*." She looked at me coyly, then slapped my hands as hard as she could.

I grabbed both her hands and pulled her toward me, and a wave of feeling flowed between us.

"You're beautiful, you know. Your eyes are so blue."

"They are still blue?"

"Uh, yes, they're still blue. Deep blue. You playing with me?"

The tension between our arms and the look in her eyes did a number on me. I really wanted her.

She felt it, too—at least, her face was flushed. She freed her hands and pulled her legs out from under her. "This is enough questions, no?"

"Okay, I guess. If you promise to tell me more later." She began to climb down from the table and reached for my hand for balance. "I've got to find out more about Camille tonight," I said, "about when she met Rodin. How about if I read and then we talk?" I slid off the table.

"All right. After you research," she said, averting her eyes.

July 14

Jesse Lucas

Research/Topic exploration for performance piece

It seems worth spending time on Camille Claudel—skimming over her would be like ignoring Johnny Depp's influence on Tim Burton, or DiCaprio's on Scorsese. Or Frida's on Diego Rivera.

I thought Camille strictly modeled for Rodin, but she was a powerful sculptor. From a middle-class family. She studied with Rodin after her teacher left the country and asked Rodin to check up on her and her English friend, Jessie. Rodin was forty-three, twenty-four years older than Camille. Apparently she was beautiful, with intense eyes, pouty mouth, a nose she thought was too big and made fun of, and long auburn hair she wore up on her head. She was stubborn and defiant—untamable.

When Rodin fell in lust/love with Camille, she basically tortured the hell out of him: avoided him when he followed her to London, even wrote letters reprimanding the poor guy for his diet. In his letters, he told her he loved her passionately, that he was on fire, that he was so joyous around her. Honestly, the guy sounded kind of annoying, constantly moaning over their lopsided relationship. But the whole time, he was living with Rose Beuret, a seamstress who started as his model, became his studio assistant, and had a son with him.

Camille eventually fell for Rodin, even though she was upset about Rose. In one letter, she wrote that she was thinking about him while nude in bed. Obviously something had changed. But she stayed fierce and independent, even compiled a list of rules for their relationship. E.g., he couldn't use female models he'd sculpted before. That seems pretty unreasonable.

It's not clear whether she literally modeled for him, but she was the inspiration for *The Kiss, Meditation, Danaïd,* and *Martyr.* No matter what happened behind closed studio doors, I still think Rodin was undressing her in his mind, using her as a "virtual" model.

More important, Camille was a talented sculptor, almost unknown in the U.S., which seems strange. Rodin's sculptures were stiffer, hers more fluid, more sensual/sexual, often in marble. And sometimes they sculpted on the same subject: her *Young Woman with a Sheaf* looks like Rodin's *Galatea.* What's up with that? Who came up with what first? Pretty interesting.

I'm really off on a tangent, but I can't help thinking that Camille's important, will add something to my performance piece. She's pulling me in. Gives the sculptures in the garden another dimension, since she inspired so many of them. Rodin's obsession with her reminds me of Jeremy Irons's fixation on Meryl Streep in *The French Lieutenant's Woman.*

*W*hile Jesse worked, it was easy to concentrate on my drawing. I sat on the edge of the table, my feet on the seats below, the sketchpad in my lap, pondering what to draw. Finally, I adjusted my grip on my pencil and proceeded to draw myself with Jesse, arms outstretched and hands clasped. I shaded the figures with the pencil's fine tip to make us look as if we were chipped from white marble. I was sketching the background of my drawing when Jesse spoke.

"Camille Claudel sounds like she was pretty controlling, when she was with Rodin."

"First, it is *Cah-mee Cloh-del*. Second, you must not speak of something that you know nothing about."

"And you do?" he said, with a half-smile.

"Much more than you. I know her life intimately."

He shook his head. "I've never known anyone who got so close to the subject they were studying." Then he lowered his voice. "Sometimes I wonder if it's even good for you."

A group of three people entered the garden—a blond man and woman, and a dark-haired man. They were quite elegantly dressed. Her scarf looked expensive, as were their shoes. Jesse and I could not stop staring at them as they moved among the statues. The blond man seemed to know the most about art.

"Do you think she is *with* both of them?" I asked.

"You think it's a threesome? That's your first thought? Wow." Jesse's voice was higher than usual.

"It does happen. But I think maybe she is with the dark-haired man."

"I think the blond guy is her brother."

"She is very, very comfortable with him. This does not always happen with people who are together."

"I guess opposites attracting is pretty accurate. Hell, maybe they're just friends, all of them. But I doubt it."

"*Oui*, there is so much energy between them, but perhaps they work together, on art."

"Like Camille and Rodin. She wasn't just his lover—"

"As so many people think."

"—she was an amazing sculptor. I've been looking at photos of her work."

"You have photographs here?" I had to see them.

Jesse found a book in his pack and flipped it open to a page with the statue *Girl with a Sheaf*. I sat down beside him, hip to hip, and grabbed the book from his hands with a ferocity that startled him and me. I lingered on each page, studying the images. My work.

"Her stuff is sometimes on the same subject as Rodin's sculptures," Jesse said. "I'm starting to wonder if she came up with any of the ideas first."

Anger ricocheted up my spine and pounded inside my head. I slapped the book shut.

"*Oui*, she did, *certainement*." I stared into space, trying to chase a memory and run away from it at the same time. I felt as if I was spinning in circles.

"Ve-ry interesting," Jesse said, staring at me. After I had calmed a bit and could meet his gaze, he spoke again. "Can I ask you something else? I . . . get the feeling that Camille was playing with Rodin's feelings, like a cat batting around a mouse that it's already cornered."

I stood up as memories of my first year with Rodin filled me. "Camille did not fall in love with Rodin for some time. She felt suffocated by him."

"Do you think he was stalking her? In her personal space?" he asked.

"He invited her to sculpt in the *space* of his studio and to assist him," I said, a bit confused.

"Not that kind of space," Jesse grinned. "Never mind. It's okay."

I tucked my sketchpad under my bench, feeling more contemplative. "Camille fell in love with him later . . . had fantasies . . . ."

"Of what?"

As the memories came, I could not seem to stop myself from speaking them out loud. "She dreamed of removing her clothing and being his model." I placed my hands on *Orpheus's* uplifted arms. "She ignored that she was from a proper family."

"I wish you'd tell me where you get all this. Your sources are probably only in French, right?" Jesse came up behind me, and his arms encircled my waist. "Did she model?" he asked.

I ducked out from under his arms and wandered among the statues. "*Oui*, Camille was his model—in private, not like the other models."

"I'm wondering how you know so much."

"You could say I was there."

"O-kay. That's one way to put it. But really, your research is obviously much deeper than mine. So maybe you can help me understand something. I get that Rodin was obsessed with Camille, but to me, she seems so territorial, so possessive, with her list of demands and all."

More memory-images rose up in my mind, and sparks, as from a fire, flared inside me. "Rodin was living with another woman. Would you like your girlfriend to make love with another man? Where is she at this moment?"

Jesse sank down on the bench. "Uh, New York City. I don't think we're together anymore." His face paled. "It was long distance. It's over."

"Over? You mean, it is finished?"

"Do you want me to have a girlfriend, Cat?"

"I was thinking it was quite permanent."

"Well, do you?"

I could not ignore his question or the quick tempo of my heartbeat. I crossed slowly to Jesse's bench and sat next to him. My throat was swollen with unspoken words. By his ear, I noticed a bruise. I bent toward him and touched it gently, then brushed my lips softly against it.

"This is my answer," I whispered, surprising myself. When he reached out for me, I slipped off the bench and tugged at his hands. A strong vibration ran from my fingers to his, and back. "We must do something special tonight," I said. "I want to give you a personal tour."

"A tour of your person?" he asked, with a teasing tone.

"No, Jesse." I tried to suppress a laugh, almost certain I understood his meaning.

"Okay, okay."

The garden seemed alive now, as memories returned to me of Rodin chiseling the statues. "These night lights that shine from below remind me of Rodin's studio," I said.

"Obviously, he didn't have lights embedded in his floor."

"He lighted his studio with candles when people came to see his work. The reflection of the light on the bronze, do you see it? This is because he did not polish his figures. They are not smooth to the touch."

"Wasn't that partly why the art world rejected him?"

I loved that he had such curiosity about Rodin. I nodded and guided him over to *Meditation,* my statue. After running my hand down the statue's strong thighs, I took Jesse's hand in mine and guided his fingers along the thin bronze seams crisscrossing the abdomen.

His eyelids lowered, Jesse inhaled audibly. He was feeling the sensuality of the bronze as I was.

Then he asked, "Aren't those lines where the pieces of the plaster cast met?"

"*Oui,* he left them." I walked Jesse over to *Eve,* and felt the contours of *Eve's* thick calves and her muscular buttocks. "Look here. It is the mark of the cloth Rodin used for drying. Here is the impression from his thumb." I drew Jesse's hand to the gouge and then across the statue's thigh. "Each mark is so expressive, isn't it?"

"Hmm." He made a low sound, almost like a groan, and I laughed quietly. I could have groaned myself.

"Adèle was the model for *Eve.* She was dark, savage."

"I can feel it," he said, hoarsely. "Her body is really powerful."

He reached for my hand and moved it along *Eve's* hip. I could feel a warmth spreading through me, as if my body were heated bronze.

"Adèle inspired Rodin," I said. "He captured her soul in the statue."

"You honestly think the model was that important?"

"The model was very important, his inspiration. Not for each sculptor. But for Rodin. Do you understand?"

"I'm starting to."

"*Orpheus* is one of my favorites." The gravel scattered under my feet as I led him to it. "Look, see the hand on his lyre. Eurydice was above him once, but Rodin decided to remove her. Now only her hand is left."

"Orpheus almost looks like a woman. I read something about Rodin reusing molds of arms and legs, no matter if the statue was a man or a woman."

Jesse knew more than I thought. "*Oui*, Rodin uses the feminine and the masculine in the same sculpture."

"Androgynous."

"There is another I love." I pointed across the garden. "It is more quiet, but so beautiful. More classic." We passed the row of tall trees.

"*Prayer*," Jesse said.

"Rodin did not call her a statue. Only a sculpture." I pressed Jesse's hand along the back of the statue's thigh and watched as his fingers spread out to cover it.

"You really do know a hell of a lot. It's amazing." He looked at me intently. "I like listening to you."

He pulled me in, and I could feel the muscles in his chest, the warmth of his skin, his hand on the small of my back. His lips were so close, then touching, pressing against mine, soft, yet rough at the same time. I leaned into him, my arms meeting behind his neck, my fingers in his tangled curls. His lips pushed on mine, parting them, and I welcomed it.

But slowly, insidiously, from the shadow-memories inside me, a ribbon of fear wound itself through my body, until I could not ignore it, until it made me pull away from him.

"Cat, what are you doing?"

"I must," I said faintly.

"What is it? What are you afraid of? I don't think it's me." He stared at me, shaking his head, his mouth a tense line.

Then he walked to the bench and slung his pack over his shoulder. As he headed toward the road, I called to him, fear feeding my imagination. "Do not look back, Jesse. Please. Remember the myth. Orpheus looked back at Eurydice and he could not take her from Hades."

"Well, this isn't hell," Jesse said, turning his head toward me. "And it's not a myth."

Crunch, crunch. Just after three in the morning, I startled out of my sleep. A man was stumbling around the sculpture garden, mumbling to himself in a familiar voice, "Goddamn cunt. They got no right. What's this worl' comin' to?"

I slid off the bench and peeked around the juniper. The man with the low voice. He had returned. It was dark enough and I had been so deep in sleep, he looked like the shadow of a man, a nightmare. My heart clenched.

He lost his footing in the gravel and leaned against *The Three Shades.* His back was turned, but his profile was in view, his skin as pale as milk in the moonlight. He was of medium build, with stringy muscles in his arms. He was real!

I slipped off my shoes and darted behind the pedestal of *Claude Lorrain,* my heart pounding against the wall of my chest.

"That bitch. Can't kick me out."

Holding my breath, I tiptoed to the first tall tree in the row of trees separating the garden. The shadowman looked down, and I dashed to the second tree, then the third. As he stumbled and lurched forward, touching a finger to the ground, I reached the sixth tree. I rested there and counted ahead. Five more.

Peeking out, my muscles turned limp to see him by *Martyr,* nearly facing my tree. If he looked up, he could spot me.

"Fucking cunt."

My heart was beating loudly, competing with his words. What will he do to me if he finds me? After these trees, where can I go? I spotted the low bushes behind *The Gates of Hell.* There. I must hide there.

Shadowman moved unsteadily to my bench.

I flitted from tree to tree and stopped behind the last one. He glanced in my direction, and I stood as erect as I could.

"I'll kill her. I'll fuckin' kill her."

Whack. He slammed his fist into his other hand, and I made a dash toward the bushes.

"She thinks she can tell me whatta do."

I leaped over the bushes, tripped, and fell onto the dirt.

"Hey! Wazzat?" He scanned the garden.

I flattened myself on the ground behind the shrubbery, watching him with one eye.

He stumbled out from behind *Orpheus* and surveyed the scene. Moving in the direction of my hiding place, he tripped and fell against *Martyr.* When he righted himself, he seemed to be staring straight at me.

"Who's here? Sumbitch, come out or I'll find ya. And you'll be sorry." He laughed and wheezed, then quieted. Neck shanked forward, eyes darting about, he looked like a guard dog trying to sniff me out. I held my breath until I felt lightheaded.

Finally forced to inhale the cool air, I willed myself to take shallow breaths, though I wanted to gasp in the air and let it out in a whine of fear. He began to stagger toward the benches, leaning on the statues for support. A tiny sound escaped from my mouth. His head twitched back toward the bushes, and I dug my fingernails into my arm.

"Cunt. Nobody messes with me."

He stopped. But then he continued making his way toward my bench and finally sank down onto it.

I crawled for three meters, away from the shadowman, through the rough-leafed bushes that were growing at regular intervals, until I reached the corner of the museum building. I could go no further. I curled into a ball to control my shaking and eventually fell into a fitful sleep, opening my eyes with a start every time I dozed off.

———— ✦ ————

The morning sun woke me, and I peered out. The shadowman was gone, but I shivered at the remnant of his voice in my head.

I am so vulnerable. At any moment, a stranger who wished to harm me could end my time here, before I even found what I had come for. I needed a way to escape from the garden.

But when I uncovered my buried bicycle, I discovered its tires were soft and flabby. I had never seen soft tires on a bicycle. If I needed to leave, I could only go on foot.

All day long, and especially as the dark approached, there was a stiffness in my face and back muscles, and I jumped at every sound and shape. I wished to sit beside Jesse, close my eyes, and rest.

But I realized I was vulnerable with him, too. My body, my feelings. And he around me. Yet, this connection between us, it seemed to be a good thing. The thought set off a longing in me. For Jesse. To be with him in every way I could think of.

It frightened me, too, for that vulnerable part of me was linked to my dark inner core, the darkest part of my past that I couldn't remember, didn't dare to remember. Would Jesse have the patience to be with me?

I tried to calm myself by thinking of his features and his body in the way a sculptor would, as if he were clay or plaster or bronze. I laughed to myself as I imagined the beautiful sculpture he would make.

I slid into a seat between Lisa and Claire. From the day Claire wore the tits-and-ass T-shirt, she never let up on that assignment. Marc Stein told us that would be her project—to dress out of character. She'd dyed the front of her hair blue since the last class, and she was wearing black lipstick. She was his example of fearless.

"We've got a lot to do today," Marc Stein said, taping long strips of butcher paper to the walls. "Body art is one of the basic categories of performance art. What videos have we seen in class that might be in that classification?"

"Chris Burden being nailed to a Volkswagen."

"That fly walking across Yoko's body."

"How many of you have run across Yves Klein's body painting in your research?" Marc Stein asked.

"The paintings with naked bodies?" This from Tito.

"Talk about it a little more."

"Well, these models are covered in paint and they roll around on a canvas and create a painting. Can we do that?" Everyone laughed.

"Nooo," Marc Stein said. "But we'll be experimenting with an art project I saw done in the UK." He held up the masking tape. "This performance is about cooperation, collaboration. In performance art, who are you in collaboration with?"

"Anyone in your piece."

"Your audience," I said.

"Divide up into threes," Marc Stein said. He turned on some classical music. Bach, I think.

Claire and Lisa grabbed my arms from either side. O-kay. This would be interesting.

Marc Stein had us stand in a line while he taped our wrists together and handed each of us a fat colored marker. I was in the middle. We headed for one of the blank pieces of butcher paper on the wall.

"Time to draw," he said. "Keep drawing until the music stops. I'll be filming, but just ignore me."

On my left, Lisa immediately started moving her hand in big loops. My hand had smaller movements in mind, and we were out of sync right away. On my other side, Claire acted more like a collaborator, and we actually started drawing wavy lines together. But that didn't last long. First of all, we were all laughing hard. And I couldn't seem to control my hands or my degree of cooperation even if I wanted to. At certain points, I just let go and went with the flow of their hands. That definitely felt the best. But it required relaxing, which wasn't simple.

The music changed every so often, and that influenced the intensity of our lines. When it stopped, I couldn't stop laughing for a good two minutes. Our drawing looked like the work of a two-year-old. Pretty cool, though.

We walked around the room, looking at each other's drawings. Even walking in sync was a challenge. Marc Stein was filming the whole time.

"Nice threesome," Tito said as we passed him. He had a guy we called *the fullback* on one side and a tiny girl on the other. The girl yanked hard on Tito's hand. "Behave," she said.

"Well put," Marc Stein said. "Moving on . . . the film of this exercise is not the product or the point of the performance. It's just a record. The experience is what counts. Keep that in mind when you're doing your projects."

Marc Stein had us sit on the floor in a circle and talk about our out-of-control experiences. He closed the session by saying, "Remember those moments when you were letting go. I want you to collaborate with your creative self in your pieces. Listen to your instincts. Don't think too much. Let unexpected things happen. Improvise."

"That was amazing," I said to my partners as we unwound the tape and became free entities again. Lisa hugged me, and I hugged her back.

As I left the room, I felt freer than I had in a while. Hadn't laughed like that or been that relaxed in a long time. I was even in a good mood at my late shift at work, even though I was disappointed I'd miss meeting up with Cat.

———— ♦ ————

The next night, Marc Stein met with each of us about our projects and then sent us off to work on them. He was hacking from a cough and probably wanted to go home and crawl into bed. I went to the garden, anxious to see Cat.

She was studying *Martyr* when I got there. The sky was just starting to let in some darkness. I knew she wouldn't be used to me showing up so early.

"Hey, Cat. How are ya?" Even though I spoke pretty quietly, she jumped at the sound of my voice.

"Hey, Jesse," she said, imitating me. "It is hard to know when you will come." She didn't sound angry, just confused.

"I really missed seeing you last night—had the late shift again. Then class was really short tonight, so here I am."

It was interesting to see her when the sun and moon were both out. The blue of her eyes was even more intense, and her hair had a reddish tint. The bronze of the statues was different, too. Their surfaces looked flat rather than shiny, because the ground lights weren't on yet.

I interlaced my fingers with hers.

"What do you do in this class you have?"

"It's different every time, but we do crazy things. Last time we were tied together with two other people and made a drawing."

"This is unusual. I would like to see it."

"The prof threw them away. It's mostly about interacting with other people in the class." I laughed, thinking about Tito's partners.

"What is so amusing?"

"There's this guy Tito. He and the prof are sort of at odds. He's a riot, though."

"Tito. I heard this name in the garden."

"No kidding."

"At night. I did not see his face."

"That's weird."

"He was passing through. Perhaps it is the same Tito."

I couldn't figure out what the hell Tito was doing in the garden, but he was pretty unpredictable. Who knew?

A car careened into a parking spot in the distance, and I looked in its direction.

"You, know, while I was at work, I was thinking about something I want to show you. It's really close by. Over there." I pointed past the parking lot. "Bet you don't know about the Goldsworthy."

"What is it?"

"Come on." I led her in front of the museum, across the parking lot, and onto hard, dry earth dotted with oak trees.

"Over there, see it? It looks like a snake, but it's a stone river," I said. "The rocks start out small but get really large at the end."

"It goes on and on. I have never seen anything like this. Who built it?"

"Andy Goldsworthy's this famous sculptor. He makes perishable sculptures outdoors, uses things like leaves and flower petals. He balanced rocks from the rubble of an earthquake that happened here. Cool, huh?"

Cat and I walked along the sculpture, weaving in and out of the sides of the stone river. The walls got so high, we could lean against them and hide in their curves.

"What is that in your ear?" she asked, staring at the wire from my iPod.

I plucked out the earbud and placed it in her ear. "Listen to this. Do you like him?"

She grimaced and pulled on the wire. "He is very loud."

"Not into Iggy? He's great. Raw, honest. I've got some of his boot-legged stuff, and an LP of *The Idiot*. The Stooges, and Patti Smith and the Velvet Underground, they're my favorites."

"I do not know these musicians."

"They're garage rock, before punk. It's great stuff, but not everyone's thing. What do you like?"

"I do not hear very much music now. I once liked Stravinsky. And Eric Satie. Both are very modern."

"Modern? Well, revolutionary, for their time anyway. Like Iggy," I said. "So we overlap in more than Rodin. We're not so *opposé*." She smirked at my French. We continued down the sculpture. "See how the rocks've been placed really carefully on top of each other? There's no cement."

"This is hard to do."

Whenever we arrived at an inner curve of the sculpture, it felt like an intimate place. The oak trees overhead and the quiet of the night, except for a little traffic hum, added to the atmosphere.

"So tell me, Cat," I said softly. "What do you do during the day?"

"I study. I survive."

"Do you spend all your time here? Is this all you study? You seem too young to be a grad student."

"It is true. This is all I study. I once worked with a master teacher. But now I study alone. What do you do in the day?" she asked.

I only got one puzzle piece from her at a time. I swallowed the frustration as best I could and let myself be detoured. "I work at the grocery store. I've got to. It's pretty fucked-up work, uh, hard work."

"Grocery?"

"Oh, you know, I basically work with food all day."

"This is wonderful." She stopped and faced me. "I love the outside market—the taste of olives, peaches, figs. And the sunflowers. I can see them in my mind, sitting on a wooden table of a Paris kitchen, catching the sunlight."

"Sounds beautiful. But, just so you know, mine's not a farmer's market. It's a CDF Store, open twenty-four, seven. I had to turn down an internship at *Funny or Die*, a chance at a small voice-over job, track team . . . the list goes on."

"Funny or die?"

"Oh, it's a website. For videos. But I have to work for the grocery store every summer, after school, and every weekend to cobble together enough money for college."

"This summer, at the market, what is your work?"

"I break down boxes, wash up garbage, stock shelves, and more of the same. The boss gets a kick out of riding me nonstop, since he knows I can't afford to lose the job."

"I understand. You do it to have an education. So, after your work, you go to your class at Stanford, and then you come to me."

She moved to the next bend of the stone river, and I followed her.

"Yes, and then I come to you. And that's the best part of my day." We faced each other.

"Is this true?"

The air was very still. I leaned toward her with a shyness I hadn't felt before. "I think you're my muse," I whispered.

"Do not say this so easily, Jesse," she said, holding my forearms. "It is dangerous."

"Dangerous? Why?" Strange—her voice was low, and there was no hint of a tease in it.

"You must understand it can be. Trust me. It is a relationship that causes harm. I know."

I pulled my arms toward me, so her fingers traveled along my forearms, and our hands met. "I don't get it . . . but I'll trust you."

"I am coming to trust you, too." Her voice was so hushed, I wasn't certain I'd heard her correctly, but the way she looked at me was different. As if she was letting me in.

We sank into a stillness, like a stone slipping through water. Then we both got self-conscious again—at least, I did—and we looked away, toward the sculpture garden.

In the parking lot between us and the garden, a girl with blonde hair slammed the door of her car, and the beep of her key-lock broke the mood. She fluffed up her hair and looked around her in every direction. My shoulders tensed as she walked through the parking lot toward us.

"Jesse. There you are."

"Lisa, what are you doing here?"

"You said in class you were doing something on the sculptures, so I thought I might find you here."

As she got closer, the dipping sun caught her hair, her short blue dress, and her dark purple toenails.

"I'm meeting somebody here for a quick dinner at the restaurant before they close," she said. "They make great homemade soups."

"Lisa, this is Cat."

She ignored Cat and continued to talk to me. I stiffened.

"So, I was hoping you could look over the outline of my class project. I'd be glad to give you feedback on yours, too. You've got my number, right?"

"Uh, yeah." I looked down.

"Okay, great. See you soon. I'd better run," Lisa said.

Cat and I headed toward the garden as Lisa strode toward the steps of the museum. Cat studied her, silent. Was she watching Lisa's blonde hair bouncing on her shoulders, the confident way she walked? Fuck.

"She's in my night class, that's all," I said. "Don't worry."

"She seems to know you quite well."

"It's all in her head, Cat. Sorry about all that. We're just casual friends, classmates. I don't really know her that well. Let's get back to what we were doing, you and me."

Cat picked up the pace, eyes straight ahead on the garden, keeping a distance between us. We walked without talking, me feeling guilty for no reason. Damn, Lisa, nice going.

"The statues look beautiful from a distance, don't they?" Cat said. Finally. I soundlessly let out air from my lips, relieved that she'd changed the subject herself. At the edge of the garden, Cat stopped by the row of bicycles. "Can you help me with something?"

"Anything," I said.

"I am having trouble with my tires."

"That's easy," I laughed. "I didn't know you had a bike."

She wrestled it from the rack, and I inspected the tires.

"I don't have anything to blow them up with," I said, "but here, we'll just borrow this." I removed a pump from another bicycle and filled both her tires with air. When I bent to squeeze them, she must have seen the back of my neck.

"What is the meaning of this?" she asked.

"The tattoo? It's a broken infinity sign. There are a lot of questions that need to be answered before anything makes sense to me."

"I like it very much."

"I like your toe ring." I wrapped my fingers gently around her ankle and slid them down to her toe.

"This reminds me of seaweed draping around me in the ocean."

"I don't know if that means you like it or not," I laughed, squeezing her ankle. After tapping the front tire, I wedged it back in the rack. "Your tires should be good to go for a while now."

"Thank you. You saved me," she said.

"I did? Such a funny thing to say."

She stood in front of me. "I am serious. You gave me my freedom." She placed her hands on either side of my face, on the stubble I didn't have time to shave. "And more than that, too." Standing on tiptoe, like a dancer, she kissed my cheeks, my lips.

I questioned her with my eyes, searching for approval this time. And when she didn't pull back, I outlined her lips with my finger, then kissed her hard and held her as close to me as I could. Our mouths were open now. I tasted her mouth and she tasted mine. She was the first to loosen her hold on me, arching back to look at my face.

But then she was kissing me again. My sense of touch was so intensified, her lips felt bonded with mine. It reminded me of *The Kiss*, but with lips touching.

"Please," she said, her hands on my chest, gently holding me an arm's length away. I let myself be pushed, but kept my eyes on her.

"I am sorry," she said. I should be alone now . . . to understand what is happening to me."

"You sure?" My voice sounded husky. I didn't want to go.

"I need for everything to be slow."

"I'll try to go slowly. But Cat, it's okay to feel something, you know. Don't run away from me. You're so skittish—like a cat, like your name. You don't have to be."

"But I do not know if . . . ."

"Here, let's just sit on the bench and watch the sky." I felt for her hand, guided her to the bench, and sat her down.

"All right," she said, nestling next to me and relaxing against my shoulder. I ran my fingers through her hair, sometimes stopping to carefully separate the strands from each other.

She didn't tell me to stop.

J woke up filled with what I might call *hope*. I drank a half-finished bottle of apple juice from the garbage and hopped onto my bicycle, ready to explore.

"*Au revoir*, statues," I said. The bicycle wobbled at first, but I righted myself and cycled off down the street. Soon the large oval and the church came into view. Cyclists sped by on either side.

I wended my way to the tree-lined path I had discovered before. Young people were chatting and laughing as they rode and walked. Everyone had somewhere to go. Some of the answers to my questions about this new life were surely out here somewhere. I pulled over to the side of the road to gather my thoughts. Maybe I would find another source for food and a place to sleep in an emergency.

"Hi, need directions?" It was a young man. He was stocky, with straight blonde hair. He seemed a bit more polite than Jesse.

"I am just looking around."

"Can I get you a cup a' coffee?"

"I would like some food with nutrition."

"Not sure food anywhere on campus is that nutritious, but a smoothie might work."

"A smoothie?"

"How about some fruit then?" He led me to the stand I had seen before and presented me with a peach and a banana on a plate made from paper. It was quite generous of him.

"I'm Nicholas. Who are you?"

"Cat."

"I'm going here in the fall. Figured it would be good to take a few classes this summer, get a head start. There's a chance I got accepted by mistake," he laughed. "What about you?"

"I study Rodin."

"Oh yeah, they have that garden."

I dug my teeth into the pulp of the peach, juice dripping from my mouth. Then I moved on to the banana.

"You were hungry. Never seen anyone eat like that. It's great."

"I need to go now, Nicholas." I wiped my lips with a napkin.

"Where're you going? We were just getting started."

"I have a lover." Once the words were out, I knew they were not completely true.

"A lover? Wow, serious."

It was serious. I thought it was. But would Jesse agree?

"Thank you for the fruit," I said, finding my bicycle and wheeling it onto the path. I pedaled to a clock tower that was two stories high and stopped. The sound of the chime triggered a memory of a Paris clock tower: a train station, the gray-white steam, the deep ring of the clock filling the air, up to the vast ceiling.

A dark-haired young woman in tight blue pants paused beside me and studied the large gears displayed below the clock.

"This is like the train station in Paris," I said to the girl. The memory was so vivid, I had to tell someone. "I had a life there. Before I was residing in a bronze body. I mean to say, before I came here." I knew I had said too much.

"Really?" said the girl. "I came to Stanford, instead of UC Santa Barbara, to be more than a bronzed body myself. Even though they had more in my major down there."

I nodded, unsure of what the girl had said, and watched her walk off. A feather flittered by my foot and I caught it. It was cerulean blue with black trim and short white tufts. I carefully settled it among my other treasures, then jumped onto my bicycle and rode further down the path. In a plaza of sorts, I dismounted to study a jagged sculpture in a fountain—it was strange but uninspiring. One hundred meters past the fountain, I smelled food.

Among the congregation of bicycles outside a large building, I left mine and headed toward the aroma of roasting meats and coffee. Inside, there was a buffet set out in a large semi-circle, so I found a plate and began piling food onto it, tasting it with a flexible black fork. Probably, I was not invited to this party. But I needed nourishment. I hoped no one would be angry.

"Hungry, huh?" said a young man with a shaved head.

"This is, uh, wonderful," I said.

"You're easily pleased," he chuckled.

As I was leaving the circular dining area, I felt fingers encircling my upper arm and tried to shake them off.

"You need to pay over there." The woman's voice was sharp and her eyes hard. I felt my face turning as pale as her apron.

"*Pardon*," I said. The plate clattered when I set it on a sideboard.

Picking up the abandoned plate, the woman shook her head at me. "What's wrong with you?"

I marched quickly toward the door, tripping on a mat. Outside, I found my bicycle. I had to go home. The food was to buy. How could I not know this? How stupid I was in this world outside the garden.

Setting off for the garden, I looked up to find myself surrounded by buildings I had never seen. Sprawling wood structures lined each side of the street. Trombones and drums played in the distance. Where was I? I turned right and left down the roadways, which became wider and wider, but I could not find my landmarks. My calf muscles began to ache, my mouth was dry, and I was becoming lightheaded. How could I forget to bring something to drink?

I had to find the building with the food, get my bearings. A feeling of panic settled in my throat.

"*Pardon*." I stopped beside a sturdy-looking young woman in men's brown boots. "The building where they sell food, where is it?"

"Huh?" the young woman stared at me. "You mean the Union? Turn left here, keep on for about a quarter mile, and take your first right into the parking lot."

"Where do I find a drink?" I eyed the clear bottle the girl held by her side. "I feel that I might faint. I need water."

The girl shifted from leg to leg. "Water? Here, just take mine." She handed me the bottle and scurried off.

I yanked at the top for several minutes, then studied the picture embedded in it and twirled it in the direction of the arrow. I had no drinking glass so I brought the bottle to my lips and gulped the water down, some of it trickling onto my clothes. When I climbed back onto my bicycle, my legs worked the pedals without so much complaint.

From the front of the Union, I spotted the fountain in the plaza and sighed in relief.

"So I joined a soccer team with chicks," Jim announced to me, Olivia, and Doris, who was tying on her apron.

"No tackling, I hope." Doris laughed. "Now you boys keep outta trouble today."

"You, too, Doris," I said. "You look hot in that apron."

"Thanks, Jesse. No touching."

She chuckled to herself as she descended the stairs, coughing at intervals. Jim winked at Olivia as she navigated around us. She did a pretty good job of pretending to ignore him.

"I don't know how she can make a uniform look so good," Jim said. "And how does she pull her hair back so tight?"

"You always talk a big game. Go for it, Jim."

"Fuck you. She must have a boyfriend."

"Whatever. That soccer league should be right up your alley, if she does."

"You wanna join?"

"Between work, school, and this girl, I'm pretty booked up."

"You still with that weird girl?"

I glared at him.

"You said she was weird."

"No, I didn't. I just wish I understood her better." I pulled at my apron tie so hard it almost tore, then mumbled to myself, "Who knows if she's even got a place to live."

"What?"

"Never mind."

Jim was standing by the assignment sheet.

"So, what's my job?" I asked.

"Whoo, boy, you've got the orange juice machine."

"Fuck, that thing gets so clogged up with crap. It'll take me all morning to clean it."

"So, that girl," Jim said, ahead of me on the stairs.

"Okay, she's a little strange in some ways."

"Like you aren't strange. Here you are headed for college and wasting your time here. You're worse than me. Hanging around a dead-end job."

"How do you thinking I'm paying for school?"

"You couldn't find a better gig?"

"They give me the longest fucking hours in town. That combined with my lifelong, bloodsucking college loans should just about do it. Hey, did you talk to Terry about a raise?"

"He says to make an appointment. What the hell does that mean? Dress up in a tux and tie?"

"Just do it, Jim."

I headed for the orange juice machine, and Jim followed behind me.

"Pick up the pace, girls. I'm not paying you to chitchat," Terry said, appearing around the end of an aisle.

When Terry disappeared, I let Jim catch up to me. "I haven't told anyone this, so just shut up about it, but she practically has one, maybe two, outfits, and . . . ."

"What? You really outdid yourself this time. She's probably homel—"

"Like I haven't thought of that?" My voice was too loud. I looked away from Jim's stare. "I'll meet you in the back room."

I wheeled the juicer to the back and took off the glass jug. All the pulp had collected and congealed inside. I got a scrub brush and started scrubbing the hell out of it. Jim was washing produce at the industrial sink next to mine.

"What else were you going to tell me about your girlfriend?" Jim asked.

"Well . . . ." I was hoping like hell Jim wouldn't tell anyone else. Things spread like a forest fire in the grocery store. Seemed like he'd always had my back, though. "Okay, so she had a weird relationship with some guy.

Like he put her on some pedestal and then things went really wrong. So I have to move super slow with her."

"You've got the patience of Job."

"What does Job have to do with it?"

"You just set yourself up for trouble. Can't you find someone normal?" Jim laughed. "Course, you'd probably be bored with that, huh?"

"I'm not bored, that's for sure."

The shitty juicer took hours, especially with Terry hanging over my shoulder, pointing out miniscule spots of rotten orange pulp I hadn't noticed.

Finally, it was time for class. First we reported on performances we'd seen online. Then we did "radically unexpected things" in our seats or in front of the class. That was the homework. About five minutes into class, I pulled out some bright red lipstick I'd found in my mother's room and smeared it on my lips—without a mirror. Everyone hooted and whistled. It was beyond embarrassing, but worth the reaction. Of course, it was impossible to wipe it all off at the break, until Lisa gave me some makeup remover that tasted like perfume. When class resumed, Tito shouted at Marc Stein for making him sit off to the side and never calling on him. Tito wouldn't shut up, mouthing off about his future and what he'd expected from the class. It was very convincing.

"Are you kidding?" I mouthed at Tito, but he didn't respond.

When Tito settled down a little, Marc Stein said, "That reminds me of that Andy Kaufman sketch in a restaurant, where he threw a fit and no one knew if he was serious or not. Look that up tonight."

So I was in a pretty good mood when I got to the garden early. But Cat wasn't there. It was weird. She'd always been there. It was as if she'd dropped out of my life, and I had no way to reach her. Pacing and constantly glancing down the road got really old. So I opened the detailed biography of Rodin I was relying on for my information.

After an hour, I'd skimmed at least fifty pages and I could feel myself heating up. I couldn't concentrate on the pages anymore and took up pacing again. I was about to give up and leave when I spotted her down the road. The blood rushed to my neck as she approached. Fuck.

She smiled weakly in my direction as she set down the bicycle on its side. I marched over to her and gripped her shoulders.

"Where have you been? I was worried." I knew my neck must be a dark red. How could she just disappear like that?

"I was riding the bicycle. I lost my way. This hurts."

I released my grip and held her forearms more loosely. "You've always been here before." I breathed deeply, trying to let it go.

But then the fire came up again. Fuck. "Ya know, this is crazy. What's up with you? It's long past time you told me, Cat. I feel like that guy in *Blow-Up*, getting closer and closer, but the girl's still a fu . . . a mystery to him. Why do you spend so much time here?"

"It is all I have, all I am interested in," she said. "My art, my study, my time with you."

"So are you majoring in art, or what? You haven't told me a damned thing the whole time I've known you."

"I am sorry, Jesse. It is so hard for me to look at myself and what my life is. My past is very *compliqué*. I do not really understand it."

"Okay. So it's obvious there's something about your life that's different, that you're afraid to tell me."

"*Oui*," she said. Her face was pale. "Can you be patient with me?"

I drew in air and blew it out, trying to calm down. "You scared me, Cat. I thought something had happened to you."

I wrestled with my backpack, pulled out a pen, and turned her hand palm-up. She made a tiny gasp when I wrote my number on the puffy part of her thumb.

"That's my cell. What's yours?" I asked. "I should have gotten it before. It's my own damn fault."

"Cell?"

"You don't have a cell phone?"

She shook her head. "I am so tired." Tears invaded the corners of her eyes. "And my sadness from the past has found a way to come up as well."

Her eyes were suddenly distant, and she gripped my arm as if remembering something frightening.

I hugged her and wiped a tear that had almost reached her chin. I settled in beside her on a bench.

"You should tell me about it." I tried to be gentle, though I could feel fear making its way into my jaw muscles. Maybe she had some horrible secret. But I felt for her, and I knew about holding onto secrets. "Can you tell me anything? It might help."

"I cannot remember it," she whispered. "I do not know that I want to remember."

I touched her cheek with the back of my hand.

"Jesse, I am just happy to be with you. The answers are here with you, in this garden. Not out there."

She curled next to me, her head in my lap. As I stroked her forehead, she drifted toward sleep.

"It's okay," I said, my voice a murmur. "Whatever it is. It's okay. It's okay." I was talking to her . . . and to myself. How bad was it?

———— ◆ ————

I wasn't able to return until two nights later. "I'm so sorry, Cat. I had to cover for someone last night."

Her face brightened when she looked up and saw me.

"I still don't have your number," I said.

"I hoped you would come back. I hoped I did not frighten you away," she said.

"No, you didn't. You couldn't. How're you doing?"

"Thank you for the kindness the other night. I know it kept you from your classwork."

"So formal," I smiled. "My homework isn't that important. If you can't tell by now, I like being with you."

"I see it."

Sitting down on the bench with me, she jiggled off her shoes and tucked her feet under her. Her toes nearly touched my leg. I scooted closer and tickled the bottoms of her feet, making her giggle and kick at my hip to free herself. Before she knew what was happening, I grabbed a foot and pretended to bite her toes. She shrieked in delight.

"Rascal," she cried, pushing at me until I stopped.

She blushed when a student with a Stanford backpack and long curly hair walked by, leading a tiny white dog that resembled a dust mop. He turned toward us and smiled, and Cat reached down and patted the dog's back.

"His name is Gordo," the boy said, making Cat laugh.

"He knows you?" I asked.

"No, of course not. He just enjoyed watching us, no?"

"Yeah, I guess." I reached for her foot again and rubbed the arch. When I glanced over at my backpack, the long thin object sticking out of the top jolted my memory, and I pulled the pack toward me. "As little as I know you, Cat, I know you've been drawing for a long time."

I handed her a paintbrush with black flexible bristles and a bottle of India ink that the man at the art store had recommended. She received them like they were treasures. Then she ruffled the bristles and playfully stroked my nose and cheeks back and forth, painting my face.

"This is so perfect, Jesse. I will use the tip for drawing and the side for the shadows. You make me spoiled. And you are right. I have been creating art for a long time." She looked off into the garden. "Too much of that time, I spent with my teacher—I was much too close to him." Her eyes widened. She seemed surprised to have spoken her last thought out loud.

"He's the one in your bad memories?"

"*Oui*, it is true. I have mostly pushed the memories of him away, but they seem to be reforming piece by piece."

I could feel a curtain closing over some painful part of her past as her gaze returned to me.

"Now tell me of you and the theater. I am curious. How did you begin, Jesse?"

I kept quiet for a minute, focused on her eyes, wanting to sit with what had just happened: She'd told me something important about herself. And, from the softness in her eyes, I could tell she knew it, too.

"Well . . . me and acting," I said after a while. "Not that many people in my life are interested."

"Tell me."

"This teacher got me into it. He used to have us do these things he called *reenactments*, of history. I was Julius Caesar, and the Black Death during the Plague. He gave me some great parts."

She nodded, playing her fingers along the tip of the brush.

"And then there were plays. I even got to be Zeus. Romeo. When I was on stage, I could be another person. It felt so damn good to be in a new skin. Like I was a snake shedding scales that were too small for me."

"I know a similar feeling from drawing. It is a place like meditation. I do not think about myself."

"Yeah, that's it. It's like I'm this other guy, like I'm living another life."

"I understand what you are saying."

"I get to feel stuff I never even detected was in me."

"It is like a new chance, a second chance."

"In a way. You get all that from drawing?"

"Well, just being here, too, when we talk, when we are together, I feel it."

"Hmm, I think you're right." I pulled her onto my lap, folded my arms around her, and kissed her gently on the lips.

With her curled on my lap, I stroked the back of one of her hands, then the palm of it. All the sensations in my body were awake.

"You have a sculptor's touch," she said.

I kissed her again, my lips touching hers just briefly. She kissed me back in the same way, and we softly explored each other's lips and tongues. The touch stayed gentle but the feeling from it whipped through my body and settled between my thighs. I knew not to push her too quickly. But my ragged breathing must have told her it was a struggle for me.

Arms around each other, we listened as the chirping of crickets broke the silence at irregular intervals.

"When I was little, I used to think that sound was from hundreds of crickets," I said. "I remember when my dad told me it was only a few."

"We call them *cricri*. I used to fall asleep to their sound when I was a child."

The snarl of a car motor and a hip-hop beat invaded the quiet. We both straightened up, and she looked at me for some explanation.

"A car radio," I said.

The music had broken the spell. She smoothed her skirt and climbed off the bench.

"Tonight you must work, no?" she asked, slipping on her shoes.

"Yeah, I guess I better."

"What research are you doing now?

"I'm on Camille again. She has a way of taking over, doesn't she?"

"I suppose so." She looked down at her feet.

"Let's talk about her once I know more, okay?"

She nodded without much enthusiasm, as if she wasn't sure she wanted to hear what I found out. Kneeling down, she found her sketch-pad under the bench, then filled a cup with water and twisted open the bottle of ink.

We both sat motionless for a few minutes. I had to let the heat seep from my body. Maybe she did, too. I watched as she diluted the ink with the water. She used bold lines of different widths to draw an old white-haired man who looked Latino. The drawing had the 3-D quality of a sculpture. I pulled myself away from her work and opened my laptop.

July 21
Jesse Lucas
Research/Topic exploration for performance piece

I checked out some more performance art the professor recommended on YouTube, but the violent or semi-violent ones were the ones that kept my attention:

- the woman who jabbed knives between her fingers—Marina Abramovic (there's an accent on the c—can't do it on my computer)
- the famous video of the guy who had his assistant shoot him in the arm
- Yoko Ono sitting on stage while people from the audience used scissors to cut her clothes

Question of the day: Was Camille in love with Rodin? To what extent? (Not sure why I care so much, but I do. It somehow seems significant.) He was so much older than she was. Rodin was definitely in love/in awe of her, obsessed with her at the very least. He helped promote her art, paid for her expenses, told other people she was "a sculptor of genius."

But even with all that, Rodin stayed with Rose Beuret. He didn't give her up to be with Camille alone. Why? Some say it was to protect himself from what he intuitively knew was Camille's unbalanced inner state. Or because Rose was the mother of his child and stood by him no matter what. Or because Rose was ill. Or because he was a bastard. Or because he loved both women—maybe they both filled different needs for him.

But did Camille love him? Her letters are so blunt and harsh—even when she's "in love" with him, she sounds superficial, like she's talking to someone who's more into her than she's into him. Flirty and teasing, but not passionate or sacrificing. I don't think she loved him with that love that poetry alludes to. Like the way Eurydice loved Orpheus, and vice versa. Like Lisa loved David in the '60s classic film. Of course, myths and movies aren't reality, but even Rachel used to write more passionately to me.

Rachel. What I had with Rachel was fun, but it was nothing like what was happening with Cat. I'd never been with someone who saw so many sides of me, pushed me, stimulated me.

*J*esse looked over to me. His stomach rumbled just before he spoke. "You hungry? I sure am. Want to grab some food?"

"Where? Where is this food?" I asked.

"You look like a hungry lion stalking a zebra herd. Let's go. Some restaurant'll be open downtown."

"Downtown?"

"We can walk."

I grabbed my hooded sweater, and he slid my art supplies into his pack.

"Never without your hoodie. Pretty attached to it, huh?" He grinned.

"Hoodie? Well, you are never without your computer."

"Got me."

He pulled me to him and guided me through the museum parking lot to a road lined with stately palm trees. I gripped his forearm and he moved closer, placing his arm around my waist and resting his hand on my hip. Boxy-looking automobiles in multicolors raced along the road beside us, and I stared at each one. When we entered the shop area, Jesse stopped abruptly in front of a building with a sign that read *Mexican Restaurant*.

"So the food is just okay here, but I'll eat anything at this point," he said. "I'll pay, too." He rubbed at his stubble.

"Are you certain?"

"This place, I can afford. I want to pay." The color of his cheeks deepened.

"Thank you."

I turned my head to watch as people passed by. The young girls had very short skirts, shorter than mine, and low tops, some that looked like brassieres. The scent of frying onions and hot peppers mixed with the outdoor air as we entered the small restaurant and wove our way through the tables.

"I think I'll get chicken enchiladas," Jesse said, studying the menu on the back wall.

"I want the same," I said, baffled by the choices. The words were in Spanish.

"Let's sit outside."

As I settled into a wicker chair, I spotted a small object by the table leg and inspected it, while Jesse cleared away the used cups with much clattering. It was a button, the milky color of marble, with four holes. I slid it into my pocket.

"So what's your favorite kind of food?" Jesse asked. His chair scraped against the cement as he sat down.

"French, naturally. *Crèpes, tarte aux fruits, mousse.* You know them?"

"I think so. It's not like I go to a French restaurant very often."

"I love *crème brûlée* as well."

"That's the crispy custard, right? I didn't know you had such a sweet tooth."

"A sweet tooth? Is this something bad?" I laughed and swiped at his cheek. "What foods do you prefer?"

"I guess Italian is my favorite. Pastas—my mom makes a mean pasta. I ate a lot of it while trying to beef up for baseball and burning so many calories. Carbs, you know."

I did not.

Jesse looked up. "Ryan," he said, addressing a tall young man who had stopped beside the table. "This is Cat." Then, to me: "Ryan and I were in a film workshop together."

When Ryan narrowed his eyes and studied me, I found myself shifting my hips uncomfortably in my seat.

"Hey, what you been up to, Jesse? You ever finish that film you were making?" Ryan asked. "Some avant-garde thing, right? About breaking points, wasn't it?"

"Uh, yeah, sort of. You mean *Approaching Zero?*" Jesse said. "That got aborted by work, but I'll pick it up again when I've got some equipment at school."

"Where ya goin' in the fall?"

"Chapman. How about you?"

"San Francisco State." Ryan leaned down to Jesse's ear and whispered. It sounded as if he asked, "Where'd you find her? What happened to Rachel?"

Jesse grimaced and punched Ryan lightly in the stomach, but enough to make him back up. "Hey, have a good one, Ryan. See ya later."

I was relieved when Ryan turned and left, muttering to himself. A waiter reached over our shoulders to set our plates in front of us, and I tasted the rice and brown beans.

"Ryan can be a real jerk," Jesse said. "Food okay?"

I took a bite of the enchilada. "A bit spicy, but good."

"Have you ever been to Mexico?"

"No, have you?" I tasted something very hot and made a face.

"Ha. A chili pepper. Eat some rice," Jesse laughed. "Some friends and I drove down to Tijuana once—not sure that counts. It was fun but not very cultural. We mostly drank beer in dark little bars on street corners, and bought cheap watches and butterfly knives at the market."

"I have mostly traveled in France, of course. Then in London, I visited with my good friend, who was a sculptor. Her name was Jessie also." The memories seeped through.

"I'd love to go to Europe, but I don't know if I'll ever get there, unless I make it as an actor or a director."

"You will."

"You think so?" A shyness made my mouth twitch a little. "You know, I almost made it to Scotland. My acting class went there and performed in a festival, but you had to pay your own way."

"Maybe someday I will take you to Europe, to Paris."

"I can't believe you said that. I'm salivating already."

An image emerged of a curtained window looking out on the Mediterranean. "One of my favorite places is Spain, by the ocean." The image sent a warmth through me, made me want to talk of the past. "So, do you have more questions of me for your research?"

"Now's an okay time?" Jesse asked.

"Please."

"So here's what I've been thinking . . . it seems like Camille didn't love Rodin as much as he loved her. Right?"

Mon dieu, what did Jesse find out about my life? I was sorry I thought to ask him to talk about it. Images seen from very close range flashed in my mind, chunks of memory dislodged by his question: Meeting Rodin for the first time in a small, well-lit studio. His arm blocking his face as he removed his black top hat. His full beard. His blue eyes searching mine with surprising intensity. His long strong fingers touching the cheekbones of the clay piece I was working on, the bust of Madame B.

"Your question is difficult to answer." Each word echoed in my ears.

"Well, what about their age difference?"

"She did not pay attention to age, after a time."

"You know, I've been looking at her portraits of him—they don't seem that flattering. Big nose . . . ."

"He was not so handsome, it is true. But his mind and his talent. He was brilliant."

"Do you think she was just using him?"

"No." It was not true. I had needed him for a teacher, but he had needed me, too.

"What's up?" he teased. "Why aren't you telling me more? You're usually pretty arrogant about what you know." He grinned and tapped my upper arm lightly to raise a smile.

"Arrogant? You say I am arrogant? And what about you?"

"Come on, tell me about Camille. You've obviously researched her enough."

He scooted his chair closer to mine. I scooted away, and he moved close again.

I stayed where I was. If we were going to have these talks, he needed to know more. Maybe his questions would help me, though they might pull up dark memories too quickly.

I tried to lighten my voice a bit. "All right, Jesse. Since I cannot seem to get away from you, I will throw you a bone. That is how you say it, no?"

Jesse laughed. "That's perfect."

"So," I said, "in 1889, Camille was on vacation with Rodin, in the land of Velasquez, as he called it, and they were often seen together—"

"I know a little about that time of her life."

"So then, you can answer all your questions already?"

"No, I don't have the answers, and you know it," Jesse said. "Their relationship is like a puzzle. I mean, what about Debussy?"

I covered my neck with my hand—for certain, it was mottled with pink. I clutched at my napkin in my lap as Debussy's face began to form in my mind—his elegance, his dark hair. "How did you hear about this?"

"Read it in a couple places. Do you think it's true?" Jesse asked.

"Uh . . . *oui*, there was an affair. He was close to her age. She ended this affair."

Jesse cocked his head at me. "So did she use these guys?"

"No, this is not how it was." There was an urgency in my voice. I wanted him to understand. "Jesse, her marble statue of lovers had been called 'the most extraordinary new work in the Paris Salon.'" My body filled with memories.

"But do you think she loved Rodin? For some reason, you're ducking away from the question."

"It is *compliqué*. It is true, her passionate love was for her art."

"So you're saying she loved him, but only for what he could teach her?"

"No," I said, trying to sort out the memories. "Of course, he taught her wonderful things—about movement and emotion in sculpture." I bowed my head for a moment, then looked up again. "But she did not grow up with love."

"I'm with you."

I was lost in the memories that were surfacing in short bursts: my brother's hand holding one side of a poetry book, and my hand on the other. The warmth in his voice as he read out loud. Over my brother's shoulder, the scorn in my mother's gaze and the stiff set of her neck. "Well, she did have love from her brother."

"Incest?"

"No! How could you think this?"

"Sorry. But, Cat, really." He leaned toward me. "Camille seemed so over-the-top competitive, so ferociously independent . . . ."

"This is wrong? For a woman?" My fork clanked against my plate as I let go of it and stared at him.

"No, of course not," he said.

"What, then?"

"Listen, my girlfriends have always been damn independent." His gaze was steady, unblinking. "And Camille seemed almost modern that way, but . . . if it was keeping her from getting close, then yes, I'd call that a problem."

I was listening with so much concentration, I almost could not hear him. I bent toward him and pushed my hair behind my shoulders. "What did you say?"

"She seemed so hard on herself, and everybody else," Jesse said. "How could she really love anyone?"

My heart contracted in my chest. "I do not know."

He spoke again, with care. "So, Camille loved Rodin the best she could?"

I nodded.

"Maybe she didn't have room for anything, anyone else but her art," he said.

Tears gathered in my throat, and I closed my eyes. "Maybe."

"Cat. Please don't take it so personally. I'm just trying to understand." He moved his chair closer and I felt his strong arms encircling me.

"I am, too," I said. "I am trying to understand myself."

*A*s we headed back down Palm Drive holding hands, her mood lightened. The vast night sky seemed to do it, along with the sounds of a brass band. The music filled the space around us, even though it came from far away.

I pulled her off the road into a circle of oak trees with muscular, low-hanging branches.

"Where are we going?" she asked.

"To dance."

"I have not danced for a long time. Maybe I cannot remember how."

"Hey, you hold yourself like a dancer all the time," I teased her.

"Do I? I think of myself as awkward."

"Don't worry. I'll make you look good."

"And you say I am arrogant!"

That made me chuckle. "Come on," I said, just as the music changed to a ballad. I held her hand lightly and guided her into a dance position. The grasses brushed our legs as I twirled her and led her around in circles, across the open space. She yipped and giggled and made small joyful sounds I'd never heard her make before. "See, you can do it. Just trust me. My mother taught me how to dance. She said it was the nicest thing I could do for a girl. Before she got sick, I'd catch them, my mom and dad, dancing around the living room to old big band music . . . . It's been a long time."

I pulled her in until her breasts were against my chest and our cheeks were touching. The music, the warmth from our bodies. I think she felt safe with me. And I felt so at home with her.

———— ◆ ————

When I walked in the front door that night, Mom smiled at me. "How was your day?" She was hand-quilting, checking the pattern forming on the underside. She always told me it was the irregularity of hand stitching that made it so beautiful.

"I'm good, Mom. How're you doing?"

"On the last stages of this one. Someone wants to buy it when I'm finished."

"It's very cool. A combo of Log Cabin and Attic Window?"

"I never saw it that way, but you're right."

She smiled at me like she'd love me no matter if I was a fuckup, a success, or somewhere in between. I kissed her on the cheek, then tromped upstairs.

I flopped back on my bed and stared at the ceiling crack that resembled a bolt of lightning. Couldn't remember what I needed to do for class.

The creak of the front door and a slam.

"You're home early." My mother's voice.

"Yeah, new owner. I may be laid off." Dad stomped around in his boots. "He's home? Not at the grocery store tonight?"

"He's probably doing homework, Carl. Carl, where are you going? Sit down and eat dinner."

He was heading upstairs. I leapt up to close the door.

"Don't shut your door in my face."

Shit.

"Sorry," I said, but I knew he could hear the belligerence in my voice.

"You're sorry all right. Who's going to support this family when I lose my job?" He was inside and standing in the center of the room. I was next to my bed, four feet away. "You going to make a living as a faggot actor?"

I squinted in disgust.

"Don't look at me like that. Think I'm ignorant?"

"No."

"Think I didn't want to finish college, start my own business? That would have solved a lot of problems." He rubbed his chin and gazed out the window. His features were soft and loose when he turned back to me. "It's too late now."

Then he moved to my desk and randomly shoved some papers, making them scatter onto the floor.

"What the . . . ?" I muttered as I kneeled down to pick them up.

"Got one year of business college under my belt," he said. "Something useful. Could have opened a sports shop."

I stood up with the pages in my hand. That's when he punched my left arm to punctuate his sentence.

I winced but tried like hell to shake it off.

"I'm working at a job right now and you know it, Dad. Lined up a job at college, too. I told you that a long time ago."

"Do I need to knock some respect into you?"

"Why don't you go eat dinner, Dad?" My voice was as soft as I could make it. I had to get him out of my room. He seemed to be moving in the direction of the door, seemed to be listening to me.

I backed up until I was at my desk, muscles tensed, and set the papers down. In the one second I looked away, he crossed the room and kicked at the desk chair. I jumped out of the way, but not far enough. The chair glanced off my leg.

"Show respect," he said, as he jabbed at me, purposely missing.

I assumed the fighting pose he'd taught me, as he played with me— getting me to block punches he never intended to land.

I felt the punch before I could block it. A right to my ribs. Stabbing pain. But it didn't knock the wind out of me. I reeled and swung back. Missed.

He slapped the side of my face. "Haven't I taught you a damn thing about fighting?" he said. "We men need to learn to defend ourselves. That's the one thing my pop had right."

He disappeared out the door. I was alone again. I went down the hall, locked the bathroom door, and nursed my ribs with a washcloth and some cold water.

*A*fter meditating several times the next day, I walked to the green oval of grass. It was studded with patches of tiny-headed wildflowers, and I picked a bouquet of pinks, yellows, and blues. The palm trees made me think of us dancing in the fields, and I began to understand what I longed for, what I searched for. Perhaps this was how I was to find the lost part of myself.

The moon was barely up when he trudged slowly into the garden, head down.

"Jesse!"

"Huh?" he grunted.

I handed him the wildflower bouquet, tied with a strand of wild grass, sitting in a paper cup filled with water.

He walked past me. When he looked up, the shadows under his eyes were blue with anger, and his cheek had too much color in it.

"What is wrong?" I asked, startled by his expression. I studied his face and placed my hand on his cheekbone. "Your face, it is inflamed. What is this from?"

"Nothing," he grumbled. He pushed my hand away.

"Nothing? Is this what you say when something happens to you? Please tell me."

"It's none of your business." He glared at me, his eyes harsh and vacant at the same time, his arms tensed as if ready for a fight.

I scrambled away from him through the statues and stopped behind the tall pedestal displaying a *Burgher*'s bust. I leaned my back against the smooth surface and sank down to the ground, breathing hard. Fear filled me like dark, thick liquid filling a vessel.

"Where are you?" he pleaded. "I didn't mean it."

I remained silent.

"I had a bad night . . . fucked-up night."

I could hear him crunching through the gravel, moving from statue to statue. When he peeked behind the pedestal where I was sitting, I shrank back and folded my arms around my legs.

"I'm scaring you? I didn't mean to." He kneeled beside me. "There're parts of my life I've got to keep to myself. I shouldn't have come tonight."

"It takes much to frighten me," I said. "But I feel afraid when you push me away from you."

He slid down beside me, knees bent, and stared at the gravel, his eyes nearly closed. After several minutes, he spoke, "My father . . . ."

"What about him?" I asked.

Nothing. Then, "He . . . ."

"He what?" I whispered.

"He takes his anger out on me."

"Oh, no."

We sat silently while I stroked his cheek, his hair, the back of his neck. I stood up slowly and removed the flowers from the cup. Then crouching, I wiped his cheek with the cold, dampened edge of my top.

Suddenly he was talking, telling me more: "He goes nuts over small things, always has. Like money. It's crazy. If he finds out I've spent any of my grocery store pay, it sets him off. 'How're you going to buy your fancy books? How're you going to make a living as an actor? Huh, huh? Don't expect me to subsidize you at your Hollywood college.' His neck turns this blotchy red, and he's out of control. Pummels me with his fists. I try to fend him off. I'm bigger than him. But he's so much quicker, was a boxer during college."

"*Mon dieu.*"

"Last night, he said he might be losing his job, accused me of not working, which is nuts. He flared up like a match, caught me in the ribs. Shit, he's ruthless. His father used to beat him, bad. Crazy thing is, I can fight off anyone else. Something holds me back with him."

"Is he a drunkard?"

"He drinks, yeah. But I'd rather have him drunk. Then he gets sentimental, says he's sorry, says he can't stand to watch me make the wrong choices."

"And your mother, does he hit her?"

"No, just me. It's been going on for years. It started when he stopped thinking I was just a kid. I threaten him somehow . . . it's crazy."

"Your mother permits it?"

"She's been sick for a while. Stays in bed or on the couch. Sews quilts to sell online. She's got Chronic Fatigue Syndrome or something they don't recognize as a real disease. Besides, one time she called the police. But the cop knew my dad from the gas station, laughed it off."

"And what of you, Jesse? How do you live with it?"

He was quiet. But he let me put my arms around him and hold him.

*T*he next night, I slid onto the bench. My words were stuck in my throat. When I did speak, my voice was muffled. "What do you do with rage?"

"I was filled with it," Cat said. "I permitted it to destroy me." She shuddered, and placed her hand on her chest.

"You okay? What do you mean?"

"I did not mean to say this," she said. "I just wanted to say I know about anger. Let me help you if I can."

"Please tell me what to do," I said. I knew my face was flushed. I had been living with this for so long, but it was stronger than ever—now that I'd let it out, told her about Dad. It was eating my insides, blocking out everything else.

She searched my face. "It seems to be very strong with you. When you hate your father so much. . . ."

"It's my fucking fault?" I knew I shouldn't attack her, but I couldn't stop.

She flinched but kept on. "No. But it will be with you always if you do not . . . ."

"What?"

"I think you must make something from it, Jesse."

"I'm supposed to forgive him?" My voice reverberated through the garden.

"I did not say this. Create something from it. It is energy, it is powerful."

"What?" I shouted. "What are you talking about?"

"If you feel all of it, if you use it, maybe you will discover more about it."

"If I let it out, I'll . . . ." I looked away. My jaw was pulsing.

She turned my face toward her. "You will what?"

"Kill him," I spat.

"I do not think so."

"You have no idea what it feels like."

"I do. I think I do."

"I'm afraid to even fucking think about feeling all of it."

"I have fear of my feelings, too," she said softly. "But, Jesse, you must . . . you can."

"How could you know?" I barked. Fuck.

"The first night we were in the garden together, I saw something in you."

I straightened up and looked at her, took in a deep breath and let it out. "You said it was important that we met that night."

"I think we are connected," she said. "That night, I saw the anger, the sadness of your eyes. I understood it. It is *la destinée* we found each other in this garden."

"You think so? Fate or chance, I don't know." I clasped her hands in mine and kissed them. When I looked into her face, I could almost see myself. "Please tell me, Cat. What are you so angry about? You can trust me."

She hesitated. Then: "It was my relationship."

"With that older guy, that mentor, right? What did he do to you?"

"We were entangled in so many ways—teacher, student, art, love. I still try to understand how it went so badly."

"Must have been pretty brutal. Can I help you somehow?"

"You are helping me, Jesse."

The clock tower chimed ten times. We both looked in the direction of the sound.

"Ten o'clock," I said. "Damn, it's getting late." I squeezed her hands and slowly released them. I rubbed my palms against my eyes. "I've got to pull it together and write about my project. My first draft's due really soon, and I can't work at home."

"You write and I will draw."

I slapped my hands lightly against the length of each of my arms to rouse myself. We sat back on the bench—shoulders, hips, legs touching, her bare foot against my calf. The tap of my computer keys and the soft scrape of her pencil on the rough paper mixed with the sound of our breathing. On her paper, it looked as if a modern-day *Thinker* was taking shape.

Inside me, everything was shaken up. This thing with Cat, it was sending me into territory I didn't even know existed. Her positive take on rage was like some foreign language to me. Revolutionary. I was so used to seeing myself as a cynic, but maybe someday I'd understand what she was trying to tell me.

July 23
Jesse Lucas
Research/Topic exploration for performance piece

Revolutionaries. What does it take to end an endless cycle? Go against the grain? Buck/fuck institutions and throw out tradition?

Rodin was a revolutionary, made critics howl: His early work was labeled *strange/unfinished/disproportional.* They gossiped about how he had nude models walking around his studio so he could observe them in natural poses. He had to show his stuff in an exhibition called *Salon des Refusés,* which displayed the indie/outsider artwork of the day—rejected by the official Paris Salon jury. Later on, they called him the "Michelangelo of the modern age," but first, they held his feet to the fire. Who else? (see bookmarks for more details):

- People came to see Manet's *Luncheon on the Grass* and *Olympia* to jeer. Both paintings are of nudes in casual settings. That was outside the box in those days.
- Mary Cassatt's father said he'd rather she was dead than painting in Paris with the Impressionists.
- Reviews of Ibsen's play *A Doll's House* called him "an egoist and a bungler," "repulsive and degrading," "literary carrion." BTW, Ibsen wrote a play inspired by Rodin and Camille! WTF? So many coincidences.
- At Stravinsky's *The Rite of Spring,* people threw food on stage.

- People were merciless about iconic musician Iggy Pop—called him thuggish and stupid.
- Reviewers called Scorsese's *The Last Temptation of Christ* filthy pornography. People protested outside theaters.
- Yoko Ono was hated for supposedly breaking up The Beatles, and her performance art was dissed.
- Jackson Pollock was called "Jack the Dripper."
- Truman Capote accused Jack Kerouac of being a typist rather than a writer.
- The Academy treated Spielberg like a lightweight for a long time.
- I love Kevin Smith's quote. Something about how people don't think he's good at filmmaking and fucking hate his guts.
- Camille wasn't rejected so much for her work, although some critics said she went too far to break the mold, said her sculpture was too sexual. She was mostly put down for her revolutionary lifestyle. Both society and her own mother called her a whore for being Rodin's mistress.

So the question is: What does it take to start a revolution, to believe in yourself so much that you can withstand pounding/ suffering/rejection/humiliation, march off in your own direction anyway, and tell your critics/the authorities to go fuck themselves? Hell, some artists weren't recognized till after they died, but they kept on anyway.

A crow landed on the picnic table next to me and nabbed a crumb, cawing loudly about his find. My fingers stopped moving on the keys. What about me? Did I have the guts to even be vulnerable—let alone revolutionary—in my acting? In my filmmaking? In class, I felt a flash of honesty in my work every once in a while. But just for a second. Everybody was going for Heath Ledger's fearlessness—I saw it in River Phoenix, too, and obviously James Dean. But for me, it was like something had me tied up and gagged, holding me back. Marc Stein pounded me for it, too. I hoped like hell I could get past it in my performance piece.

*W*hile Jesse worked, I wrestled with the memory that surfaced when he talked about his rage. The memory-image was sharp: My uncombed hair falling from a clasp. Eyes feral. Body twisting and lurching around a room filled with human shapes.

It had been hiding in the darkest corners of my mind, festering, waiting for Jesse's words to stir it up. I could find no sense to it, just terror. When I tried to push it back down, it stuck to me like black tar.

It only eased a bit when I took out my drawing materials, held the brush in my hand, and smoothed out the paper. I worked on a sketch of Jesse as *The Thinker* in clothing. With each line, the act of drawing guided me slowly back to the present.

When Jesse spoke from behind his computer, the sound of his voice startled me. "Cat, you said Rodin was insecure, doubted himself."

"*Oui*," I said, finishing a brushstroke along the thick calf of my *Thinker*.

"How'd Rodin have the balls to break with the way things were going in sculpture?"

I set down my pencil, and a pleasant memory took form in my mind: the sureness in Rodin's hands manipulating and gouging the clay, the way he held his neck slightly forward when he sculpted, the squint of his eyes as he judged his own work.

"At nineteen, Rodin knew he needed to sculpt," I said. "It was a seed inside him. Insecurity does not always stop people."

"He doesn't seem like the kind of guy who'd have the required backbone."

"Backbone?"

"Guts, courage."

"Then you do not see all of him."

"Okay, but—"

"Jesse, he did not find success until he was forty years old. He had doubt, but he kept on. And he had help." I reached back in time. "From his father . . . from Rose."

Rose, the woman Rodin lived with. My stomach clenched into a knot. I wiped her image from my mind as quickly as I could.

"But he still needed to keep going all those years, not knowing what would happen," Jesse said. "How the hell did he do it?"

I put my finger to Jesse's lips. His eyes made him look like a wounded animal, desperate for help. The muscles of his jaw were clenched. When I placed my palms over his jawbone, the prickle of his stubble woke the sense of touch all over my body. "Shhh," I said quietly. "You will not understand everything by thinking. Let me help you."

The garden was empty, and the moon above was slim. I took Jesse's hand and led him toward the opposite side of the garden, behind the shrubs by *The Gates of Hell*, all the way to the corner of the museum building.

I stood facing him, without speaking, and studied him. Then my fingers were on the buttons of his shirt, undoing them one by one. As I unbuckled his belt, he took in a breath and held it.

"I want to discover how you feel, how you look, how beautiful you are. This is all, Jesse. I want you to understand it—how a sculptor sees the human body."

I undid his sandals and jiggled them off one at a time. I pulled down his khaki shorts. He closed his eyes and made a low sound. Then I removed his underwear, and my body longed for him. I moved quickly to his face and navigated it with my fingers—his eyelids, the frown lines around his mouth, the cleft in his chin. I moved down his chest and arms, around his shoulders, cupping his shoulder blades, as if I were sculpting him with my fingers.

"You can see . . . I'm going crazy," he said.

"Please let me understand you in this way. I want to show you how the artist thinks. It is not only in the mind. He feels the shape, the volume, in his hands, in his heart. The clay, the plaster. It is alive to him."

"O-kay." He sucked in his breath, and I breathed deeply, too.

"I am a sculptor today only." My hands followed the shape of his hips.

"Jesus, Cat."

"Shhh, Jesse. You have a bruise here on your arm, a scar on your rib. I think on your neck, too. No?"

"From him."

I gently touched the bruises and scars, then ran my hands along his chest and stomach muscles, down the backs of his thighs, over the hairs on his calves, and all the way to the high arches of his feet.

"You are beautiful, as I thought you would be." I closed my eyes briefly, feeling the desire built up in my body, but I remained still.

He stayed still, too, while I admired him in the moonlight, and then he slowly dressed.

"What about you?" he asked. "Do I dare ask? Can I . . . do the same with you?"

"*Une autre nuit.* Another night."

———◆———

Another night came. The moon was still slim, but a bit plumper. Holding Jesse's hand, I followed him behind the bushes, and we stood facing each other again.

"Okay?" he asked.

I nodded.

He knelt down and gently removed my ballet shoes from my heels and toes, then my socks, first orange, then blue. He unzipped my skirt and slipped it off my hips, and rolled my tights down my legs. He pulled my lacy top up and over my head and arms. I felt his fingers moving up my calves, my thighs, squeezing them gently as if they were clay beneath his hands. He stopped and put the back of his hand lightly between my legs, and I became instantly warm there.

"Not now," I said.

He continued up, kissing my navel. "Your skin is so pale under your clothes."

I moaned. "No kissing. Only touch. Be a sculptor, Jesse. I am made from clay."

"No, you're not," he said, letting out a whoosh of air from his lips. His fingers felt my breasts, then the muscles in my forearms, my upper arms. He traced my eyes, my nose, my lips, my ears. He ran his fingers through my hair, all the way to the ends. I could barely remember how to breathe.

"Uuuh. I can't stand it," he said.

"I think it is time to dress," I said. I pulled on my tights, my lace top, and my skirt as he watched.

"I've got to take a breather. I'll be right back." He headed toward the small fountain, and I could hear him sputtering and mumbling as he splashed himself.

When he returned, I was facing the gates. I reached out for one of his hands, loosely interlocking my fingers with his. With my other hand, I brushed some of the water from his face.

"What is your surname?" I asked.

"Lucas."

"Jesse Lucas, what a beautiful name. It fits you."

"Only when I'm here. Nothing remotely beautiful fits me out there. I actually like myself when I'm with you."

I was humming when I entered the garden the next night and caught sight of Cat sketching on her bench. Just remembering her naked body made my skin tingle. I rested my hands on her shoulders and peeked at the page. With a pencil, she'd laid down some sketchy lines for a drawing of a naked man and woman. She was thinking about us, too.

"You've got so much talent," I said.

"What is the song you were singing?"

"So you heard me, huh? 'A Change Is Gonna Come.' It's a Sam Cooke song."

My phone vibrated in my pocket—a text from Tito. *Can u send me the syllabus before next class. Lost it. Lost my keys. Losing my mind next.* I laughed.

"What makes you laugh?"

"Tito's always on the edge. It makes me feel like I'm not the only one."

"This name again. I love this name."

"Yeah, he's a cool guy. He's doing his project on graffiti art, I think. Course, it's illegal."

"He sounds very interesting." She began to shade in the upper body of the man in her sketch.

I gathered her hair, pulled it to one side, and bent closer to her drawing. "Damn. You have such an unusual style. No matter what materials you use, it looks like sculpture, and it's so sensual. Not sure I've ever said that word out loud before. But it fits."

"I am happy you like it. You know, I am nearly finished with the papers in this drawing book."

"I'll buy you a new one tomorrow." Then, under my breath: "Someday I'll have the cash to buy you anything you want."

"The new paper is the only thing I need, Jesse. You must write now, no?"

I walked around and joined her on the bench. The way she tilted her head at me made her look a little shy, even scared. Probably from getting naked together—we were definitely on new ground.

"I need to finish my drawing of Paolo and Francesca. You know, they are the lovers *illicites* from *The Kiss*."

"I don't recognize that pose you've got them in."

"I made this up from my imagination. It is after they began their love affair. I wanted to show them reading their book again with each other."

"I wonder what they're reading." I laughed.

"It is the story of Lancelot and Guinevere."

"So you know? Incredible. Those two were lovers *illicites*, too."

"This is true. Your French is interesting." She barely stifled a laugh.

I inspected the drawing again. "It's us, isn't it? Your drawing looks like you and me."

"Maybe." She kept her eyes downward. "You need to work. We can talk after."

"You can't shut me up that easily. I brought you something." From a side pocket of my backpack, I pulled a lavender-colored rose I'd bought. I fluffed the petals on the side that looked a little flat.

"It is beautiful and so unusual."

"Like you."

She smelled the rose, then pressed her lips against mine. "Mmm. I like the smell of both of you together."

I draped my arms around her and couldn't stop grinning. Out of the edge of my eye, I spotted something yellow peeking out of the dirt under the bushes. A tennis ball. Her forehead wrinkled as she watched me grab it and brush the dirt off.

"Let's play," I said.

"I do not know much about play."

"Come on. Over in the field. I'll show you."

"Is it like *futbol*? Do you kick the ball?"

"Oh, you mean soccer? No, not like that." I found her hand and pulled her toward the field, giving her no room to protest.

On the ground, I nudged at fallen branches with my feet until I found a sturdy one. She picked up what looked like a tiny piece of wood and slid it into her pocket. Interesting.

"There are four bases," I said, using my foot to dig out bald spots in the dirt. "After you hit the ball, you run around to each of these places. And try like hell not to let me tag you."

"I am not certain I understand."

I laughed. "Don't worry. Stand right here. When the ball comes, just swing at it."

I handed her the thick branch, positioned her hands around it, and headed toward the pitcher's mound.

She frowned.

"Okay. Here's how you swing." I came up behind her and guided her arms through the movement, my hips behind hers. She laughed and nestled into my body.

"Now I understand," she said.

I pitched the ball, and she swung and missed. The ball stopped in the underbrush and I retrieved it.

"Keep your eye on the ball. Don't think about anything but the present, and that ball."

She murmured to herself, something like: "The present. I want it to go on forever."

When I pitched again, the branch connected with the ball—a pop up. I pretended to fumble with the catch.

"Run! Run around the bases," I yelled. "Hustle."

She ran from one spot to the next, giggling and shouting, slipping on the grasses and picking herself up. I laughed and pretended to lose the ball again, sprawling on the ground.

"Home run!"

I ran to her and lifted her up until her waist was against my chest. She bent her neck down to kiss me.

After I hit a few balls and cracked the bat, we walked back to the garden, holding hands. A couple of times, I brushed the hair from her face, just to look at her.

"Now we can get to work," I said, grinning, "now that we've played."

I opened my computer, and she flipped through her sketchpad.

"I feel a lightness in me," she said.

"You just need to have more fun. I can help you with that, for sure."

As soon as I opened the file I was working on, the subject of muses came to me. What a loaded topic. Seemed like everybody had one.

July 28
Jesse Lucas
Research/Topic exploration for performance piece

Camille was the perfect muse for Rodin—more confident than him and a rebel in so many ways:

- single female sculptor with strong ambitions
- woman from a respectable family who had what people called a bohemian lifestyle
- mistress of a famous artist—went to parties, on vacation, on business trips with him, even though people gossiped about them

Of course, in the end, I'm getting the idea that being a muse didn't work out, at all, for Camille.

What about Jackson Pollock's wife? Was she his muse, or did she just keep him from going off the deep end while he splashed paint in his brilliant way and drank himself into oblivion? She was a painter, too.

That woman who married George Harrison—Pattie Boyd. He wrote "For You Blue" for her, but she had an affair (?) with Eric Clapton and left Harrison. Bad move.

Can't forget Picasso. He had a whole series of muses. I think two went crazy, and two killed themselves. The last one was Jacqueline.

Tarantino calls Uma Thurman his muse, although he says they were never lovers.

Carly Simon and James Taylor might have been each other's muses in the '70s, until he got too fried on heroin.

Who was that woman who was an actress and modeled for artists a long time ago? Her millionaire husband shot some famous architect who paid to fuck her when she was a teenager—shot him in the face at Madison Square Garden (?).

The muse business can get pretty messed up.

Interesting thought: They say Camille was the inspiration for *The Kiss*, which is based on a story in Dante's *Inferno* about Paolo and Francesca, whose affair landed them in hell. On top of that, the book they're reading in the sculpture is about another affair gone wrong, Lancelot and Guinevere. So, coming back around, did Rodin sense from the beginning that his affair with Camille wasn't right for him? Who knows? I'm probably overthinking it. All my acting teachers say it's a bad habit I have.

I looked up from my writing. What about Cat? She honestly felt like my muse. She stretched me so much, and had this mysterious quality to her. Exciting.

And maddening. Even when she told me about herself, it didn't add up. What did she really do all day? Did she live . . . here?

My jaw clenched. I needed to pin her down. What if she was so secretive because she had another boyfriend? Like Rachel did. Fuck.

I was silent for a time, thinking of ways I could force her hand without scaring her away or making her feel bad.

I didn't realize I was staring at Cat, until she spoke. "What are you writing about? You look at me with a scowling face, as if I bit you."

I shook out my arms, trying to shed, or at least ease, the grip of my paranoia. "I've been thinking about muses. Obviously, Camille was Rodin's muse. Maybe it is dangerous, like you said."

"So you agree now? It took you some time to understand."

"Yeah, I can be a real slow learner, but I'm seriously looking at it now." I saved my file and shoved the laptop into my pack, a little too hard. I dug my fingers into the back of my neck, my temples, the top of my head. That felt better.

"Listen, there's a band on campus I was going to check out." I set her pad on the bench and pulled her up. "Come with me."

"Am I dressed well enough?"

"You look fantastic. You always do, in your outfit." I waited a beat for her to explain her wardrobe, but that was just wishful thinking. I pulled her toward me by the waist. "Here, let's take a picture, Cat."

I stood beside her with one arm around her waist and the other stretched out in front of me, holding my phone. "There." When I showed her the picture of us, her eyes widened.

"Now, let's take some with a statue," I said. "You lean against *Orpheus* the way you did when you were teasing me."

"I do not tease you."

"You've got to be kidding."

I positioned her arms on *Orpheus* and took a photograph. Then I started climbing into the lap of *Caryatid with Urn*.

"You have no respect for the statues," she said, pulling at the waist of my jeans, but I continued to nestle myself onto the statue's left leg, my hand under the urn.

"Just take the picture. You'll like it once you see it. Find me and press your finger on that button in the center."

"You do look amusing," she said, laughing. "But I do not approve."

I clambered down, and our heads touched as we viewed all the photos together.

"I look . . . ."

"Beautiful, ex-o-tic." I kissed her lightly on the lips. "Hey, let's get going. We need a change of scenery."

"All right," she said hesitantly, and grabbed her hoodie.

As dusk settled in, we wandered down the campus streets, past the wooden fraternity houses, past the bookstore, until we got to the place I wanted to show her.

"This is kind of a detour," I said. "Hope you don't mind."

"This is a children's school, no?"

"Yep."

"I like the mural of fantasy animals on the wall."

I helped her over the low mesh fence and freed her skirt when it caught on one of the metal loops.

"I love playgrounds." I leaped from the top of the fence, then spotted her as she climbed down. "Maybe because there were playgrounds wherever we moved, and they all had a similar look."

I held a canvas swing seat and invited her to sit in it, then settled into the swing beside hers. We pumped our legs in unison, and her hair floated behind her, then shifted forward, nearly covering her face. I kicked off my shoes, and she copied me, her ballet-slipper shoes flying high and dropping with a *pumph, pumph* in the dry sand.

"I suppose I did not play as a child." She smiled at her bare feet.

"Higher, go higher," I said, extending my legs even farther toward the sky, catching the air in the crook of my legs. She did it, too, and whooped with a high-pitched sound.

"Now jump," I said.

"I cannot."

"Sure you can."

"I will fly so high. And then I will come down."

"The sand is soft."

"I am afraid."

"It's fun. Just relax and let go. I promise you won't get hurt. Would I lead you astray?" I teased.

"*Oui,* you would."

"Okay, listen. We'll count to three."

"I do not know if I can."

"Come on."

"You must count in French."

"Cat, I don't know French."

"Then we will not jump."

"Oh, hey, maybe I do know. *Un, dos, trois.*"

"*Un, deux, trois,*" she said, "but still, I do not—"

"Ready, set," I shouted. "*Un, deux, trois,* jump!"

We flew from the swings. The cushion of sand gave way as we landed and fell backward, inches from each other, limbs splayed. Our laughs were deep, and we turned our heads toward each other. I reached over and cradled her face in my hand. I bit her lower lip as tenderly as I could, and then kissed her more deeply.

As we lay back again, she said, "The sky is falling onto us, the stars seem to be so close. They are just as they looked on a beach in France, long ago."

"Really?" I plucked a small cloth object from the sand. "What's this?"

"Oh, just my sack of things." She sat up and snatched it from me, wrapping her fingers around it.

"Can I see?" I sat up, too.

She hesitated, still gripping the bag, motionless, studying me. Then she turned one of my hands palm upward and placed the worn violet bag in it.

I loosened the ties at the top and peeked inside. My fingers were too bulky to take anything out, so she laid her hoodie flat on the ground. I gently shook the bag until it was empty.

Slowly, I separated the objects and spaced them evenly. She could barely look at me, as if she was waiting for me to make fun of her. So I moved very slowly.

The wooden triangle caught my attention first. "It's a perfect triangle. Equilateral," I said. I'd seen her pick it up in the field.

"I love the symmetry." Her voice was a sliver of itself.

I nodded and placed the triangle carefully back onto the hoodie, confused, but hoping she wouldn't snatch her things away.

"A penny." I fingered it and turned it over and over.

"The president, no?"

"Um, yeah, more than a century ago."

"Oh, of course." Leaning toward me, she put out her hand for the coin. She held it between two fingers and showed me the writing. "The word *One Cent,* it is backwards," she said.

"I never noticed that." I took it from her and turned it around, "Oh, I think you had it upside down."

"Ah, *oui*." She looked to me for reassurance that I wasn't laughing at her. I did feel like laughing, but in a tender way.

"A button," I said, setting down the coin and studying the button.

"It is very like the color of marble."

"Is it?"

She handed me a tiny black shoe. "My favorite."

"This doll's shoe reminds me of you." We both looked up. It was very quiet, with only the sound of a night insect buzzing nearby. Glancing at the shoe again, I said, "It's sort of nostalgic, isn't it?"

"Nostalgic, *oui*."

"It even has a little bow like your shoes." I laid the shoe on the sweater, picked up the feather by its stem, and brushed the tip along her palm.

"A work of art, no?" she asked.

"*Oui*," I said, smiling. The smell of roses wafted over to us from a cluster of yellow roses outside the fence.

The silence was very loud again in the playground. She inhaled and her body seemed to relax.

Last, I picked up the spring and compressed it between my fingers.

"It has movement, like a drawing or a sculpture," she said.

I set the spring next to the feather and held her hands. "Cat, what are all these things about?"

"I found them. It is my collection." Her face was flushed. "These are my treasures."

I squeezed her fingers. "You amaze me." A little catch in my voice. "I don't understand you, but I'm rethinking how I look at everything."

She sighed in relief. Then, one by one, she tucked each object back into the bag, adjusting the feather so it wasn't bent. The bag disappeared into her pocket.

I wrapped my fingers around her bare foot. "I'm glad you showed me, Cat."

"I'm glad you did not tease me," she whispered.

Getting to my feet, I offered my hand, pulled her up, and brushed off her back and bottom. Even after the sand was gone. She laughed and brushed me off, too. Then I wove my fingers through her hair and shook it as gently as I could, to let the sand out.

"Do you still want to hear the band?" I asked.

"Of course," she said, her voice strong again.

We strolled back down the streets, past the fountain, past the Student Union, and into a small dark café I liked. The jazz sound that hit us at the door had a sad quality. As we wove our way to a round table in a corner, someone waved at me.

Lisa.

Even though I didn't wave back—just smiled a little—Cat's eyes moved from me to Lisa. My stomach tightened.

"I'll get us some drinks. Be right back," I said. I returned with two glasses of red wine. "Showed them my fake ID," I said, so only she could hear.

"What must you show them? I do not understand. You are certainly old enough."

"You've got to be twenty-one here. There aren't any limits in France, right?"

"I have been drinking wine from my father's cup since I was five."

"What a different world. Here they let you drive at sixteen, join the army at eighteen. I mean, they really expect soldiers to stay sober twenty-four, seven?"

"How old are you?"

"Nineteen."

"You do look older than your age."

"How old are you?"

"Uh, eighteen, I believe."

"O-kay."

"It's confusing. I lost track of the years."

"Wow." That was strange, like everything else. "You know, sometimes I feel like an old man, other times I feel like a kid."

"I know this. You make me feel like a young girl at times." As she took a sip, I couldn't stop watching her lips against the glass. The wine was going to my head. "Tell me, Jesse. What is this place?" she asked.

"They book bands from this area, and the artwork is mostly by students, I think."

Cat looked around at the small, unframed canvases. They were landscapes with green skies and blue trees.

"Maybe you could show your work," I said.

"Maybe. But I must do more drawings first."

She seemed to kiss the glass as she drank.

"Whatever you say." I found her hand under the table and rested our clasped hands on her thigh.

"So, we can talk about muses, if you like," she said.

"Okay, sure. Where were we?"

"Who are the muses you know?"

"Well, I was thinking about Helena Bonham Carter and Tim Burton. She's been in so many of his films. And she lives with him." I could tell she wasn't following what I was saying. "There's Zelda and Fitzgerald. She was a writer, too, but her stuff wasn't so good. Never mind the fact that she went certifiably crazy."

"Poor woman," Cat said, letting go of my hand.

"Who can you think of?" I asked. "You don't seem thrilled with my examples."

"Well, Rodin admired Victor Hugo and his mistress, Juliette Drouet." She scooped up a few almonds from a white bowl on the table.

"What's their story?" I asked.

"Victor saw her in a play. She put aside her acting profession to devote her life to him."

"Never knew that. Interesting," I said. "What about Frida Kahlo and Diego Rivera? They created some major drama that kicked each others' butts . . . sorry about the language."

"I have never known you to be sorry for your language," Cat laughed.

"Yeah, I guess not, and I'm even polite around you."

Behind me, I felt fingers on my shoulders. "Where have you been keeping yourself, Jesse? Never see you after class anymore." I turned my head. It was Lisa.

"Right, uh, Lisa, you've met Cat." I rubbed the stubble on either side of my chin. How much more awkward could it get?

"So what's new?" Lisa asked, looking down at me.

"Not much."

"Listen, call me some time," Lisa said. "I miss hanging out."

"Yeah, uh, huh. Nice to see ya," I said, trying to wind it up.

"We could catch up before next class." Lisa turned to go. "Come early."

Cat watched Lisa walk away in her tight brown skirt, and then we were left staring across the table at each other, Cat frowning.

"You've got to know, I'm not a player, Cat."

"What is this? A player?" Her elbows were on the table, her chin resting on a fist.

"Someone who goes with more than one girl at a time."

"You had a girlfriend before . . . ."

"I was almost positive she'd dumped me when I met you. Honestly."

"I remember," she said. "But this girl tonight? Lisa." She made *Lisa* sound like a dirty word.

"I swear, she's nothing to me."

Some guy in an apron replenished our almonds. Each of us reached forward. When our hands bumped inside the bowl, we both laughed a little, expelling some of the tension.

"What were we talking about?" I asked.

"The idea of a muse," Cat said.

I relaxed back in my seat. "Yeah, it's fascinating. What about Camille and Rodin? What kind of muse was she?"

"With Camille and Rodin, you must understand." Cat's eyes were intense, a darker blue than usual. "She wanted to be successful as a sculptor, not just Rodin's student or muse. This is most important."

The band started playing a danceable jazz number. I grabbed Cat's hand. Even though she resisted, I pulled her to a small dance area beside our table and held her close. "Seriously, it's very important," I said. "And it's very intriguing. There are so many different roles for a muse . . . ."

"What are you saying?"

"Well, I read Picasso got along best with Jacqueline of all his muses, because she was devoted to taking care of him."

"Someone must be like *that* to be a muse?" She squeezed my fingers too tightly.

"Cat, I'm just exploring this. I'm basically agreeing with you—for once—that this muse thing can get pretty screwed up." I smiled and purposely cocked my head, to get her to lighten up. "I'm just saying that it may work better in cases like Jacqueline's." I twirled her and waited until she was facing me again. "Don't jump all over me, but Camille's brother said she was pretty much the opposite. Independent, willful, unsociable . . . and violent."

Cat tried to wriggle her hand out of my grip, but I held on.

"Say what you want, but Camille was not going to serve Rodin," she said. "Never."

I let go of her hand and followed her back to the table.

"Okay, I hear you. I'm thinking muses, or co-muses, either burn out or really want to be artists themselves. Or have trouble when something isn't equal to their partner—their work, or their success." I knew I had a point, but somehow the whole topic triggered her, bad.

"This has some sense to it," Cat said, calming down a little.

"Or it seems like their passion for their work can get in the way of their relationship. Like in Camille's case."

"Muses cannot have passion for their own work? You cannot mean this." Her cheeks flashed pink.

"I'm just saying that if they're so obsessed with their work, they maybe can't pull themselves away from it to think of somebody else. Even if they want to."

"Why must they think of someone else?" she asked. "*Toujours*, always, women must think of someone else."

I probably should have stopped but I didn't. I spoke slowly, knowing I was on sensitive ground. "I'm talking about if they want to get close to someone." I settled back against the chair. "Besides, all muses aren't women."

"Who are the men?" She folded her arms.

"Gotcha there. I actually read some articles about it," I said. "Alan Ginsberg had guy muses, like Jack Kerouac. Alfred Hitchcock had Cary Grant. I'd say Heath Ledger, from things I've read, was Terry Gilliam's muse. And John was obviously Yoko's muse."

"I do not know of these people."

"You know, John Lennon and Yoko Ono." She shrugged, and I pushed gently on her arm. She was obviously kidding. "Even Sappho. She was inspired by male muses, and women," I said.

"Sappho. I know her poems." She turned quiet. When she spoke, her voice was close to a whisper. "I will think about what you said . . . about Camille."

I quieted down, too. "Okay, great. So we do agree on one thing: I won't call you my muse."

"Good," she said, finally smiling.

The members of the band finished their last piece and thanked everyone.

"Want to go? I think they close soon."

She folded the remaining almonds into a napkin to take with her and stood up. At a nearby table, a guy with dark, straight hair falling in his face was staring at Cat. I gave him a look and put my arm around her shoulder.

"You know him?" I asked.

"No," she laughed. "I do not know anyone."

"You'd better not be someone else's muse," I muttered to myself.

*A*fter the café, when I was alone, I sketched figures from *The Gates of Hell*, mostly from the left side of *The Thinker*. My page was covered with quick thumbnail sketches of bodies sprawled across rocks, bending backwards, groping forward. I was too tired to sketch anything from the other side, but I noticed a loose rendition of *Meditation* in the top tier of the gates.

What is the story of this figure? I will ask Jesse. Rodin never told it to me, or I forget.

In the moonlight, I washed my hair in the drinking fountain, using petals from the bright pink flowers that grew in the field and smelled like perfume. But all the while, my insides were on alert, my muscles tense. I slipped out of my clothes, then splashed water under my arms and down my breasts to bathe. It was two o'clock in the morning. I could tell from the clear chime of the clock tower in the distance.

A sound. In the gravel. Adrenaline coursed through me. The shadowman! I crouched in the doorway next to the fountain, and shivered from fear and from the cold. I could not stay there. Naked, I climbed over the wall next to the fountain, scratching my legs on the rough cement, scrambled to the bushes behind *The Gates of Hell*, and lay on my stomach in the dirt. I slithered between the shrubs like a snake in the desert, the rocks raking over my bare stomach. In the farthest corner, in my hiding place next to the museum, I lay still, eyes wide.

More sounds from the gravel, but no words. He was quiet this time. I hid for hours, my ears my only defense.

When all sounds stopped for another hour, I crept out and scanned the garden. No one. Covered with grime, I returned to the fountain and washed again, tending to the scrapes on my stomach and legs. Then I dressed and meditated and curled up on my bench, waking every few hours.

————•————

The following night, I heard the scraping of the gravel before Jesse came into view.

"You were here last night." He faced me directly, his breathing jagged, his voice as sharp as a chisel.

"What?"

"Were you here all night?" His voice was a black monotone. "Were you here the night before? And the night before? Do you do this every night, Cat?"

A quiver ran down my spine, and I held my breath. "You were in the garden and you did not speak to me?"

"Why would you be parading around like that in the dark?"

An image of my bath flashed through my mind. Oh, no. "What are you saying?"

"You're. Fucked. Up."

"You do not understand, you imagine I am—"

"Meeting some other guy." His words dug at me like claws. His jaw was hard set.

"You think I . . . cheated."

"You said it."

"Leave! Do not insult me in my garden."

"This is public property. You can't kick me out."

"I can!"

He balled up his fists. His eyes were slits, his mouth a tight line.

"What? Will you hit me now?" I jutted my neck forward, my muscles tensed.

"Fuck you, Cat." He stepped backwards.

"Go away!"

"You made me think . . . my God, you're not even sorry," he said.

"Everything you say is twisted! Every word!"

He spun away from me, and I watched as he tromped off, leaving tracks in the gravel, his fists still clenched.

He betrays me. I hate him! He has no understanding. I swiped at tears of anger that blurred my vision as I stumbled through the garden, pushing at each immovable object—the statues, the bench, the can of garbage that rattled in its cage.

Exhausted, I lowered myself onto my bench, the wood as hard as stone.

My heart aches so deeply. Will it ever stop? Why did I trust him? Why did I open up to him?

I pulled my legs up onto the bench and clutched them to me for what seemed to be hours.

———— ◆ ————

I noted the full moon and kept count, as day after day passed by. Soon it was seven days of living with the rawness around my heart. I wanted to lose all feeling, but my heart wouldn't allow it yet.

The old man with the Spanish newspaper returned with a woman who seemed to be a nurse. He had a cane, and she had to help him to the bench. He read the newspaper, and I read a museum announcement I had retrieved from the trash, describing an upcoming exhibit of paintings saved from a flood in New Orleans. The man and I lifted our eyes at the same moment and smiled.

"How are you?" I asked.

"*Muy bien, gracias,*" he said in a scratchy voice. "*Cómo está usted?*"

"*Muy bien, gracias,*" I said, copying him.

I needed his company, and I knew it was all the contact I might have. It would have to be enough. I knew I would not permit myself to love so deeply again. Ever.

After a visit of less than an hour, when the old man shuffled away with his nurse, a young child skipped into the garden with his father. First they drank juice from bottles and ate lunch packed in brown bags.

I was relieved to be distracted, to watch the boy build castles from mounds of white gravel as his father contemplated the statues. The boy looked a bit like Jesse must have looked as a child. But I pushed those thoughts away by concentrating on the boy's green eyes.

He waved at me.

"Hello," I said, glancing at his father, who nodded his approval. "What are you building?"

"My sand castle," he said.

"Can I help?"

"My sand castle. Mine."

"Of course." Young children were like that.

Soon after, the boy climbed onto his father's back and waved goodbye. When the roar of their automobile faded, I spotted a round blue object in the gravel by the boy's castle. I inspected it, noticing the trees reflected in it, and my own face, so tiny I could not distinguish my features. I carefully tucked it into my bag of treasures, which was almost full.

If I was to live in this garden with only smiles and waves from the visitors, then I had to find more about my history. This life, it could not be for nothing.

I strode across the gravel and mounted the stone steps of the museum. Ignoring my image in the thick glass door, I pulled it open with both hands and entered the marble lobby. A wooden rack on the reception desk held a display of large art books on Rodin, along with folders of information. *Sample Only* was printed on the book covers, in oversized letters. A thin, bony woman with short gray hair perched behind the desk.

"May I look?" I asked.

"Of course, dear."

People passed in and out of the lobby as I scanned the books and leafed through the loose pages about Rodin's sculptures. Finally, I found a page on my statue. It explained that Rodin used *Meditation without Arms* to bring to life a poem by Baudelaire, "Beauty." Rodin described the statue as complete and whole. He admired it as one of his best, and even called it his most perfect.

So he thought my statue was perfect. He never told me this.

In *Rodin's Art*, a book by a man named Elsen, I looked up *Meditation without Arms*. This Elsen, he said that many believe the torso was of me. This was true. The next words flew at me like a wild bird: He said the shape of *Meditation* showed that I was pregnant, and must have had at least one abortion.

I covered my face as a memory surfaced in my mind: I saw myself holding my naked belly and weeping.

"Are you all right?" the woman behind the desk asked.

I pushed the book and folders toward the woman's hands and fled from the lobby, down the stone steps, across the gravel, back to my wooden bench.

Love was so hard to understand. It was so filled with pain. Faint body-memories flickered inside me of my last days with Rodin, and from the twinge in my chest, I knew something dreadful had come of it.

Had I made this return to life only for more pain? I could see that my new love for Jesse was just a reflection of the old one with Rodin, like a sculpture recast from the same mold. I was thinking love would help me to find the part of myself I lost. But it was not true.

Head bent, I sank down and let the bench support me. Soon, I was pounding the wood, and then my thighs, with the palms of my hands, as pain turned to anger, and back to pain, on and on.

I did not notice the day going by, but then the trees were black-green. The day had turned to night.

*S*hit. Everything with Cat was completely fucked up.

Standing outside the locked classroom, it got worse. Right after Marc Stein went to get a key, Tito arrived.

"Hey, newbie." He flashed a smartass grin and pushed me in the chest, "How's it hangin'?"

What a fucker. I pushed him back, hard. Made him stumble backwards. "Think you're better than the rest of us? Huh, Tito?"

"You got a rod up your ass? What's wrong with you?"

He headed toward me. I pushed him back on his ass. Jumped on top of him.

"Fuckin' crackhead?" he shouted. "Get off me, *puta*."

Arms around my chest, pulling me off of him.

Marc Stein in my face. "Do this again, you're out of my class. You've got a lot to prove now, Jesse."

I turned my back as everyone shuffled through the door, raised and lowered my shoulders, exhaled enough anger to enter the classroom. I sat as far from Tito as I could, and I didn't hear a word Marc Stein said. Except when he quoted some famous acting teacher saying that the biggest cliché we buy into is of ourselves. That we have this narrow concept of who we think we are, but we're capable of so much more.

Encased in my car after class, I howled and screamed at everyone, at no one, at myself, behind closed windows. Maybe I was actually capable of murder. Or of being the biggest fool on earth.

What a night to have the late shift. I grabbed my apron and bounded up the steps, hoping Terry wouldn't catch me coming in late. Jim was up there, reading *Sports Illustrated*, eating a sandwich from the deli that he could barely get his mouth around.

"You're in luck, Jesse. Terry's in a good mood. Wish I'd talked to him about my situation today. He won $10 on a scratch and sniff."

"At least something's going right for somebody."

"Hey, 'sup? You don't look so good, dude."

"Turns out this girl is cheating on me. She's . . . ."

Jim set down the magazine and stared at me. "You caught her with some guy?"

"Not exactly."

"What does that mean? You found somebody's jockey shorts in her pocket?"

"Fuck off. She was waiting for someone. Meeting someone to . . . ."

"O-kay. You saw the guy?"

Doris and the girls came up the steps.

"I can't tell you all the details, or you'd really think she's nuts," I whispered.

"Seriously, Jesse, I think *you're* nuts."

"It's so great to know you're there for me," I snapped.

It was almost therapeutic to hack the stems off the old broccoli and slice it into small bunches. Except that I cut my finger at one point and bled all over the produce. I tromped to customer service and got a Band-Aid from the first aid cabinet. Didn't even bother to wipe the blood off the knob.

I had hours to myself behind the rubber doors. The more I thought about it, the less sense it made. Was she really waiting for someone? A boyfriend? Jim had a point. I never did see anyone. Why the hell would she be there naked? She'd have to be insane to be running around like that in the garden. It wasn't safe. It was outrageous. What was she doing by the drinking fountain? She was completely wet.

I took the hose from the sink and washed down the counter. Put on some gloves and stuffed the rotten broccoli into a garbage bag. Then I dragged the bag to the dumpster out back and heaved it in. A few yards away, a new clerk at the store was washing his face with the hose. Water dripped from his chin, and he wiped his wet face with his apron. I stared at him.

"Oh, my God," I said out loud to myself, as the dumpster cover clanged shut. "Oh, my fucking God."

———— ◆ ————

After work, I drove to the garden. I couldn't see her anywhere. I rubbed at my jaw, and looked around.

There she was. She was sitting on the bench closest to the museum, looking down. I headed toward her, lifting my feet to keep the gravel from snarling at every step.

"Will you talk to me?" It was hard to get the words out. Shame had settled in my throat.

She flinched, but kept her eyes down.

"It was a shock for me," I said. "I jumped to conclusions. Like I always do. But this time I really hurt you."

She stayed silent and stiff, bracing herself on the bench with her hands.

"It was insane . . . so hard to watch you. I thought you were with someone else." I kneeled in front of her. "I've been thinking you must be living here for a while now? But then when I saw you naked, I thought you were . . . . You must have been washing yourself."

She let my question sit in the air. Then:

"This is my home."

I could feel a coldness traveling out on the backs of her words, pushing me away.

"Cat." I wasn't even sure my words were reaching her at all. "I'm an idiot . . . to misunderstand you like that . . . to get so angry."

Silence.

"How did this happen to you, Cat?"

Her voice was stripped of emotion, but her face was flushed. "My fate is strange. There are things I am to learn in this life. I am put in unusual circumstances to learn them."

"What do you mean? I don't understand. You have no family?"

"No, no one alive."

"But what about friends? Don't you have someone who could put you up?"

"I am solitary. I must take care of myself."

"This is unbelievable. I had no idea. I'm really worried for you. What if someone came, at night, who could hurt you?"

"A man came . . . ."

"What the h . . . ? What happened?"

"I found a place to hide. He went away."

"We've got to find you a place to live. I've got to help you."

"Help me? I do not want your help. The only sadness I felt here, true sadness, is the night when you said I betrayed you." She looked up at me, swallowed hard, and turned her head away.

Cautiously, I sat on the opposite end of the bench. "I am so sorry I did that. It was so wrong." I reached out to touch her arm, but she cringed away from me and sprang to her feet.

"I need to protect myself. I will not allow your words to soften me. I cannot do this again."

"Please let me in, Cat. I know I made a really ugly mistake. Sometimes I feel like I *am* a mistake. Please. Can you forgive me?" I reached out to her, involuntarily.

She marched to *Martyr*, where I couldn't touch her. "I cannot. I will not." Her jaw was set. "You cannot understand. The men in my lives betray me. Each man in his own way."

"Cat. Please don't put your baggage, your history, with some other guy on me."

Her body was shaking so hard, I could see it. Her voice was low and powerful and seemed to come from someone else. "I cannot lose more of myself! I do not want madness again!" She clenched both sides of her head and squeezed her eyes shut, as if trying to ward off something painful that was rising up in her. Something I'd provoked. When she opened her eyes, she slapped at a pyramid of stones someone had left on the pedestal of *Martyr*, sending them stinging to the gravel.

I walked over to her, stopping a yard from her, waiting, praying she would change her mind. Almost wishing she would hit me, and then forgive me.

"Go away, Jesse," she yelled. I felt like a wave was pushing me away from her, a wave that was building inside her. Then, in a whisper that hurt more than any of the harsh words. "Let me be alone."

I walked away as fast as I could, so I wouldn't go back and grab her to me. The world seemed to be reduced to emotion and sound. My sandals slapping on the road. My car engine. My heart pounding . . . and then aching.

———————•◆•———————

Days later, as I walked up the steps to Wallenberg Hall, I glanced behind me at the dark path leading to the garden. A sick feeling filled my gut. It was my fucking fault. Jesus, maybe Dad was right—I was impulsive. I jumped into things, I jumped to conclusions. And now I'd lost Cat. I kept trying to tell myself it was for the better. No drama anymore. She was too strange. But all I could do was feel the hole inside me.

I settled into a chair as Marc Stein turned over a large sheet of paper on the flip chart. Tito and I avoided each other's eyes. "What is performance art? Let's at least take a stab at it. You've done some in class, you've seen it online. What is it?"

People blurted things out:

"It's performed live."

"Experimental."

"Done in public," Tito said.

"There are no rules."

"Unscripted."

"Usually," Marc Stein interjected, "but if there is a script, it's often filled with actions, not with dialogue."

"It can be body art. The performer can use their body as the performance."

"It can cause a spectacle, be shocking."

"It can be about pain, endurance."

"Can be visual."

"Or sounds."

"Place and time are important."

"Out of place."

"Can be political. Or comedy. Or serious."

"The audience is random."

"But what about Yoko and the clothes cutting?" Claire asked.

"People went up and randomly took turns."

"Okay, this is a good start," Marc Stein said. "Now, here's my feedback for each of you." He gathered up a pile of papers and passed them out. It was our journals—our explorations of our topics, so far.

His writing was scraggly and hard to read, but the gist of it was that I needed to think about my audience. Would there be one? He called my idea original. Said to be careful not to script it too much, to let it happen. Across the bottom of the last page, he'd written: *Time to make it personal, vulnerable. Been pounding this into you since day one.*

He was probably right on all counts. And it hit me that it was going to be really hard to research in the garden anymore. I'd have to go there for filming only. Maybe someone from class could help me.

As I headed away from the classroom, Lisa caught up with me. "Hey, Jesse, walk me to my car. I'm afraid of the dark."

"Yeah, right." She wasn't scared of anything. "Okay, sure, where are you parked?"

She pointed way in the distance. "In that parking lot on the other side of the oval. Got here a little late." She moved closer. "So you're not rushing off to the sculpture garden?"

"Not tonight."

We walked along the path that ran down the middle of the grass.

"Listen, Jesse, I've got free tickets to *The Dark Knight*. Want to come with me?"

"That movie's on my list. Haven't had time to see it."

"The whole thing'll be my treat. We could get some dinner . . . ."

"Lisa, I have to level with you. I'm not looking to . . . date anyone right now."

"No problem. We'll just go as friends. We'll call it research. I hear Heath Ledger's performance is like performance art."

Damn. All I needed was another girl.

But I did need a friend.

And she seemed to back up right away when I made it clear what was going on with me.

———————— ◆ ————————

Lisa met me at the entrance to the theater. She was holding a medium bag of popcorn that smelled freshly popped, munching on one piece at a time.

"Hey, Jesse."

Her hair was straighter. She had tight black pants, boots, and a purple tank top. A scarf was twisted in an interesting knot around her neck. I was going to have to be careful.

She led me to two seats near the middle that she'd saved with her belt. Watching the movie was easy, except the two times our hands touched in the popcorn bag. When the screen finally went black and the credits started rolling, I looked over at her. "What'd you think?"

"Awesome. It was all about Heath."

"I didn't really love the rest of the movie. But what he did wasn't even goddamn acting. It was something beyond that," I said.

"I hope it's not what pushed him over the top."

"People've been doing dark parts forever."

"That's true. I don't think we'll ever know. Want to get some gelato across the street?" She pointed to a narrow, well-lit store.

I'd always wondered about that place. "Okay."

We discussed the pros and cons of the flavors for a long time, with Lisa asking for one sample spoonful after the next. She decided on spumoni, which I hate. I ordered pistachio.

Part of me was relieved to relax with someone who had a regular family and a place to sleep and didn't misunderstand basic American culture.

I wasn't all there, though. I was good for surface conversation. But part of me hadn't shown up at all.

———— • ————

A couple nights after *The Dark Knight*, I found myself sitting with Lisa on the soft grass of the oval. I wasn't stupid. I knew it was a slippery slope.

I didn't want to see myself as a player. And I was too raw, anyway. So when she sat a little too close, I leaned back and folded my legs in front of me. And she shifted back to her original position. I got the feeling she wouldn't push it twice in one night, so I relaxed after that.

"I think I'm going to cut my hair for my performance piece. In public," she said.

"Are you kidding?"

"It grows back."

"No shit. Really? I can't see you going through with it."

"Got ya goin', didn't I? I'm just going to wear a realistic wig and hack my hair off that way."

"O-kay, that sounds a little more probable."

"Gets to some of the stereotypes about female beauty. Everyone always says it's rampant in L.A., in the magazines. But it's here, too. Felt it my whole life."

"Yeah, it's damn near everywhere," I said. "By the way, where do you live? You grow up around here?"

"On the main drag, University Ave. I'm living at home for the summer. Then I'll move to a dorm here."

"You grew up in one of those mansions?"

"Yeah, I guess you could call it that."

"How is it, going to college in your hometown?"

"I'll find out in the fall, but it's not too bad. I can do laundry at home. My parents don't hover. Too involved in their work. They're both entrepreneurs. Besides, my brother's applying to colleges this year, so they give most of their attention to him."

It struck me that she'd just told me more than Cat had disclosed. Ever.

After I walked Lisa to her car and was heading back to mine, I realized I'd been sucked into Cat's world, hadn't been able to see how bizarre it was.

Then, without warning, I felt the loss, a dull pain in my chest. Felt how attached I was to her on a deep level.

But it didn't matter. I couldn't be with someone with such a grim history that she couldn't open up.

Back and forth I seesawed, until I felt completely messed up. When I found my car on the other side of the oval, I just sat there, windows down, the night around me. I yanked out the papers in my glove compartment and grabbed the pack of cigarettes I'd left there a while back. Lit up for the first time in a while. Who cared? Cat had made it clear she wanted me to leave her alone. I had to do whatever it took to get away from that relationship, or whatever it'd been. I had enough trouble in my life anyway. It wasn't good for me.

I'd go to the garden one more time to film, get someone like Claire to film it for me, and then never go there again.

*A*fter I sent Jesse away, I spent days quieting the dark voices that had risen inside me on his last night in the garden. Slowly, I shut out the ghostly images of dread and sorrow from my past life. Slowly, the dark voices withered and shrank to a murmur. But I did not dare close my eyes for several nights, for fear the hidden memories might claw their way out.

On the third night, I finally slept. When the sun appeared above the horizon, it brought with it a sense of unfamiliar calmness. Now that Jesse was no longer with me, I could stop forcing myself to forge an opening to whatever I had locked away inside me. It was a time of closing down. A numbness took over, a comfortable, yet unnatural numbness.

Days passed, with at least a handful of sunrises and sunsets, and I barely remembered going about my routine, although I knew I had, for my stomach was not growling for food and my hair felt clean to the touch. I never focused in on the statues around me—after all, they never changed their positions. Seated on my bench, I barely acknowledged the people who came and went, came and went.

People crisscrossed the garden, stayed to take photographs, had picnics. They didn't seem to notice me anymore, and to me they all seemed the same. Until at least a week later when I recognized the voices across the garden, in front of the gates. The lesbian couple.

"You drive me cra-zy. Can't you call if you're going to be late?" the short girl said.

"You're too possessive," the tall girl said. "A control freak."

"Bullshit."

"Bitch."

"You're calling me a bitch?"

They burst into snorting laughter and bumped shoulders, leaning into each other. One hand found another, and they headed out of the garden.

"Just bear with me until this class is over," the tall girl said. "I'm doing everything humanly possible."

I could hear them laughing all the way into the distance, until they sounded like two birds tittering in the sky.

I glanced down at myself. A shadow of a girl. I might as well have been inhuman, a statue.

It was time.

Time to do something.

I crossed to the field and collected long strands of grass in varying hues. On the picnic table, I separated the colors into piles and wove a pattern of yellow, brown, and green, forming the beginnings of an eating mat. Maybe a pillow would be next. My fingers were so hungry to create.

I began reading newspapers abandoned on the benches, and followed a story about a man who was brown as the statues and a woman with a toothy, open smile, both interested in being president.

Days later, I even walked due south with a bag of food and a half-full bottle of water. I thought I saw a totem in the distance, and it was true. Wooden totems loomed before me. I wandered through their midst, stroking the back of an alligator, touching the chipped wooden breasts of the female sculptures. In each piece, there was so much earthy energy.

Another afternoon I ventured past the totems, until I came to a large circle of trees with a dark-colored lake in their center. Rowboats dotted the water. Birds with red wings reeled above me. I sat in the dry grass and watched the couple near me, reading books, their backs to a tree trunk. I spotted a family on the opposite shore, eating on a blanket.

When the sun was at its height, I removed my skirt and waded into the water in my tights, then dived in and swam until my arms ached. The sun was strong enough to dry me and my hair on the shore.

In this way, I fashioned a plan for each day, to fill the hours and to ward off the mourning I knew I needed to do, for him. But at night, surrounded by blackness and the hope of the stars, grief traveled through my body searching for my heart, where it lodged until the sun came up again.

One day, a pigeon from the restaurant tottered over to *Martyr* and burbled at the head of the statue. I pulled out my sketchbook to capture him on paper. It was time to draw again. I rubbed my hands over the chocolate brown cover of the pad, enjoying its rough texture, then opened it and flipped to a page.

Jesse's portrait. It was a three-quarter view, showing his strong chin. His eyes, drawn in great detail, pulled me in, releasing my feelings the way wax melts out of a mold when casting bronze.

I turned the page. Jesse holding both my hands in his, our arms outstretched. A wet spot spread on the absorbent paper, where I had sketched Jesse's chest. I looked up, certain I would find a bird. But, no. I was crying. Slowly, I turned another page. *The Kiss*, a barely-disguised drawing of Jesse and me. I pulled the pad to my breast and let the tears wind their way down my cheeks, like the ribbons of water that snake away from a creek when it cannot help but overflow.

———— ♦ ————

I heard my own footsteps on the road that night, though I hardly made a sound in my soft ballet shoes, and soon I found myself at the top of the green oval of grass. I made my way to the steps leading to the sandstone buildings, where I sat down on the hard granite and crouched there in the shadows, watching each person who passed by. Some were alone, some in pairs, grinning, chatting, laughing over private confidences, but I recognized no one.

Though I asked myself over and over why I had to do this, a part of me would not listen to such questions. I returned the next night, stationing myself at the far left of the stucco buildings, seated on a different set of oversize steps. After the clock tower chimed the half-hour for the second time, I startled to see the back of Lisa's head and her distinctive blonde waves. I stood and followed her down an arched walkway, keeping five meters between us. Lisa led me to him.

He was standing beside a wooden doorway in the stone building, waving for Lisa to join him. Lisa quickened her step and stopped very close to him. He said something to her, and she pushed him in the chest, making him laugh, as smoke traveled up from their conversation. He glanced my way and looked at me over Lisa's shoulder. Into my eyes.

But his eyes were distant, as if there were no road connecting us, as if we were from different worlds, as if he didn't know me, as if he had never known me. I forced myself to turn around. My heart sounded louder than my shoes meeting the surface of the stones along the walkway. It was many steps back to the garden.

I slumped on my bench, boneless as a ragdoll. My chest ached as if I had been punched. I had done this myself. There was no other person to blame.

I looked up and felt a pull toward *The Gates of Hell*, covered with its sea of suffering figures. One by one, I studied them—the desperate father *Ugolino*, the contemplative *Thinker*, the sorrowful *Falling Man*. I understood the expressions on their faces, their writhing bodies, the core of each figure's grief. I felt a part of them, a part of their story.

Footsteps down the road. My heart jumped and I slowly turned to look. The shape was a man, a young man.

I studied him closely, but I could see that his shoulders were not broad enough, his stride too short. He nodded at me as he passed, and I turned back to the sea of bronze figures.

Footsteps on the road again. I did not look this time. The footsteps grew louder, then turned into a trudging sound through the gravel.

"Are you playing games with me?" I stopped in the gravel near the statue of *The Three Shades*.

"Jesse?" she whispered.

I was silent.

She turned and walked closer to me. We were no more than four feet apart. "No," she said, looking directly into my eyes.

I kept my gaze half on her, half on the statues behind her. I couldn't let her drag me into her world again.

"Why did you come to campus?" I asked. I felt my eye twitch.

"To tell you . . . ."

I lowered my head and stared at the white gravel, sorry I'd come.

"To tell you that I forgive your anger . . . on the night you thought I betrayed you . . . to tell you that I was afraid."

I shook my head. It was all so familiar.

"You are such a mixture of gentle and angry," she said softly, almost to herself.

There was nothing to say.

"I came to ask if you could forgive me, Jesse, for making you go away from me."

I closed my eyes to find the words, then opened them and made myself look at her. "Cat, I never know what I'll find out about you, if anything. You've kept so much from me. I know almost nothing about you. Nothing." I ran my fingers over the stubble on my chin. "That may work for you, but it doesn't work for me." I stared at her, unblinking. "And I never know when you'll push me away."

177

It was so still, I could hear us both breathing. She said nothing.

I looked over my shoulder and down the road, my jaw muscle tensing. The raw sound of the gravel skittering under my feet scratched against my insides as I left.

I half expected to hear her calling me back, but she didn't.

The crunching of the gravel stopped.

I turned to face her, my arms hanging limply at my sides. I could see her features in the light from the moon.

"I'm afraid, too," I said.

Silence.

"But . . . I can't stop myself from forgiving you, Cat."

I watched her walk toward me. Then she wrapped her arms under mine and around my back. I could feel her heartbeat, and mine, and my whole body relaxed into hers.

"I love you, Jesse."

"I love you, Cat."

We stood in each other's arms, just breathing, for a long time.

———— ◆ ————

After class the next night, I found her by *Orpheus* and lifted her off the ground with a hug. Letting her down, I focused on her eyes to keep her from looking away. "Cat, please, I've been thinking. You living here. That scares the sh . . . that scares me. You have to let me fix it."

"I like to live here. This is the place I feel at ease. I have a history here."

"I could find a friend with an extra room. There's got to be something. Please let me do something for you. I want to."

"I am happy the way it is."

"But how'd you get here? You've barely told me anything about it. What happened? I'm not backing down this time." I guided her to a bench, brushed away some leaves, and sat facing her. "We'll never get closer if you don't trust me."

"You will not believe me. I do not know if it is good," she said. "My memory is opening and closing like the wings of a butterfly."

"Give me a chance to know you, Cat."

She hesitated for several long minutes, while I tried to reassure her with my eyes.

"Jesse, I can tell you my story, but it is a hard story to tell."

"I don't care."

"You will care. It will change everything."

"You have to tell me sometime."

She held my hand and began very abruptly, as if forcing herself to speak. "The second day of July . . . something happened in this garden. From one of the statues, the spirit of a girl emerged. She had lived her life once before . . . ." Fear rose up to my throat. Cat's eyes were shiny with tears. "The girl, she was here to repair the wreckage of her past life. She was here to find a part of herself she had lost. She met a man in the garden who was her age. Slowly, she found the courage to open her heart, and . . . ." Her voice dropped to a whisper. "That girl is me." I tried to stop my body from shaking. "I know about Camille and Rodin because in my past life I was . . . ."

"Cat, I know you feel strongly about Camille—"

"Jesse, it is true. I warned you. I said you would not believe me." Hiding a clenched fist by crossing my arms, I gulped down any words I might say. Cat was hugging herself. "Remember when you touched the statue that night, the first night, and it was hot?" she asked. "I could feel your presence. I did not emerge yet." She tried to read my face, but I did my best to cover my feelings. "Why did it burn your finger? Why was the statue filled with heat? Remember? Did this happen to you ever before?"

My mind searched in every corner for some logic, trying not to conclude that she was mad. Then she was speaking again.

"After you left, my spirit emerged from the statue. I became alive again."

Oh, God. I wanted her to stop.

"Remember how I hid behind the pedestal? That is when you returned and gave me your shirt."

I expelled bursts of air from my lips, to keep from jumping up.

"Think of everything I have told you, Jesse."

I sifted through my memories of our time together, looking for a shred of reason. I stood up, bumping against her leg.

"Not everything in this life goes with logic. I found this out the day I met you, Jesse."

I could feel my insides igniting. I had to get out of there.

"Thanks for telling me all this, Cat . . . I've got to be alone . . . to think." My voice was so low, I hardly recognized it.

I navigated through the gravel, down the road. As soon as she was out of sight, I was babbling to myself, grabbing at clumps of my hair and pulling till it hurt.

How could I be so stupid? How could I believe her this entire time? Fuuuck. Fuck this whole thing.

I felt the whack of my fist punching the palm of my other hand. The sting felt good. At least the pain was real. I headed for my car, yanked open the door, and slid onto the dingy seat. My insides reverberated with the growl of the engine, and the car fishtailed as I made the sharp turn onto the driveway leading away from the garden. I turned left on Palm Drive. The palm trees looked like sentinels, watching me leave. When I neared the end of the long row of trees, I suddenly swerved in a wide U-turn and parked the car on the side of the road.

I sank down, head bowed. "This can't be true. She's crazy. I'm a fucking idiot. What am I supposed to fucking do?" I pounded the seat beside my legs and slumped forward, yanking on the steering wheel as if I'd pull it out. This is what I deserve. Falling hard for this girl when every sign said she's fucking crazy. I'm an asshole. I had it coming. All along.

I jumped out of the car into the wild grass and thick oaks. Temporary barriers were set up to lead cars into some upcoming event. I grabbed the nearest wooden horse and threw it as far as I could. And another and another, until my heaving breath stopped me. I bent over, ready to barf. Then I reared up and shouted at the top of my lungs, "This is so fucked up. It hurts so bad."

When I opened my eyes completely, my gaze shifted to the dark sky. I could see the moon, a crescent above the palm leaves. I stood still and watched it. Sometimes it looked like a sliver, sometimes I could almost see the whole moon, faded, like a ghost of itself.

Nothing made sense. Not the moon, not my life, not that crazy girl in the garden. Everything had been there in plain view. The mismatched socks, her clothes, no family or friends. Why did I let it go so long? I could hardly see the moon anymore, my eyes were blurry.

"Cat," I whispered.

Was there some way through this, even if she was nuts? Would she hurt me, kill me? Probably not. She wasn't cheating on me. Could I pretend along with her? Fuck. I stood there on the grass for God knows how long.

I found myself driving slowly back down the row of trees, toward the moon. It followed me, or I followed it.

When I walked into the garden, she was still sitting on the bench in the same position as if frozen, hands on her lap, eyes closed tight.

"I left you once," I said softly, so I wouldn't startle her.

She shivered and opened her eyes. I sat down beside her.

"I'm not doing it again," I said.

I fell silent, my thoughts cast inward, trying to piece us together again. It was hard to breathe.

She waited for me as I wrestled with myself.

"You're here in front of me now, Cat. No matter what this is all about, I want to help you."

We sat in silence. There was nothing more to say. My body tensed, as disbelief invaded me, and then relaxed, in waves. When I'd settled down, I gingerly drew her toward me and folded my arms around her, more and more firmly.

———— ◆ ————

The waning moon was still a crescent as I approached the garden after class. Cat was by the *Caryatid* statue, feeling the shape of the urn with her hands.

"I'm in this with you, Cat."

She smiled.

"You know, this morning, I thought of food. At least I can help you with that. Then we'll see what's next."

"Food sounds wonderful."

"Let's go together, right now, and get you some."

"Where do we go?"

"You'll see. It'll be good to get out of the garden for a change, get a little dose of reality."

With my arm draped gently around her waist, I walked her slowly to my Dodge Colt, which was parked on the other side of the museum. Seeing it from her point of view, it looked like hell: faded maroon color, rusty along the bottom, covered with a layer of dirt.

"I did not know you had an automobile," she said.

"It's kind of embarrassing, a real clunker."

She glanced inside. In the back seat lay my beat-up leather jacket, two empty beer bottles, the shirt I had given her, and discarded papers. I lifted a pile of books off the passenger seat and placed them next to the jacket. The book on top was *Rodin: The Shape of Genius*, my favorite. Cat stared at it intensely. The cover showed Rodin with white hair, flanked by a pair of large dogs.

"That book is the best of any I've found." My voice turned sarcastic. "But I guess you already know everything in it. Shit . . . sorry." I looked down and let my frustration fall off of me. "Let's just get some food, okay?"

"Okay," she said. "I am ready."

"Hop in. You can put your feet on those papers. They're old."

The car sputtered and bucked.

"Tell me where we are going," she said. "When do we return?"

"You're about to find out about my world." I felt more like myself again—it was good to be in the driver's seat, literally.

Cat craned her head and watched the garden disappear from view. As we entered Palm Drive and merged into a stream of cars onto El Camino, her head turned from one side of the road to the other. She seemed especially taken by the large billboard advertising Stanford sports. On the narrower streets we wound through, she studied everyone on the sidewalk, mostly dog-walkers. Finally, we entered the nearly vacant parking lot where I parked the car in my usual spot off to the side. The motor coughed.

When the glass door of the grocery store opened on its own, Cat froze. I laughed and guided her through the opening. "Never seen one of those, huh?"

Inside, we pushed a cart together toward the far end of the store, to the produce section. I was at home here. She paused at each aisle we passed.

"I will take one from each," she said, surveying the mounds of nectarines, oranges, and apples. "Jesse, they look so perfect. Are they fresh? From open-air markets?"

"No, they're chilled and trucked in." I cupped a nectarine. "People don't realize some of these're never going to ripen—not in this lifetime. But this organic section's not a bad place to start." I inspected an apple. "We're going to have to think this through. You need food that won't rot outside a refrigerator."

"Where will I keep it? You must bring me fresh food each day." She pushed teasingly at my ribs, then pulled me to a stand overflowing with apricots and peaches. "These grow in the summer. They must be fresh. Look, white peaches. How elegant." When she bent over to rescue an apricot that had fallen to the floor, I pinched her.

"Jesse," she squealed.

"Just couldn't help myself," I said.

"Jesse, what are you doin' here when you don't need to be?"

We both turned.

"Hey, Jim. They switched your shift today, huh? This is my girlfriend, Cat. I like your beard, bro."

"I feel like I already know you," Jim said to Cat. "Jesse's been talkin' about you."

"He tells you about me?"

"All the time. Can't get him to shut up." Jim winked at me.

"Thanks, bro." I laughed.

"Any time."

"So, Cat, this is Jim. I work with this sorry dude."

"Really nice to finally meet up with you, Cat." He turned to me. "Listen, Terry's been on my tail all night. I better get back to work, or at least pretend to be productive. I've got an appointment with him after my shift." He lowered his voice. "And a date with Olivia. Life's lookin' up."

Cat and I watched Jim disappear behind the rubber curtain.

"Jim and I usually work at the same time. Great guy, keeps me sane, gives me a lot of grief."

I went back to squeezing fruits and finally had two full bags that met my standards. At the deli counter, I ordered, "Two pepper-turkeys on Dutch crunch with the works, and half a baked chicken."

"The works?" Cat asked.

"Mayo, mustard, onions, pickles. You'll like it."

Cat helped me place the food on the checkout counter—it startled her when it hummed forward.

"Thank you," she said, tapping my upper arm as I emptied my wallet to pay. She took control of the cart and pushed it out the door, which swung open and surprised her again. I followed her out.

Two men who looked like they'd wandered over from the bar across the street were approaching from the shadows, smoking.

"Nice tits, bitch," one said as Cat walked out.

"I'd fuck her," said the second man.

Cat stumbled as I grasped her arm and pulled her behind me. Swiveling in the direction of the second man, I yanked him upright by the front of his shirt. "What did you say?"

"Jesse, what are you doing?"

My right fist connected with the man's nose, making my knuckles reverberate like hell. His face transformed into my father's face. I punched him on the cheekbone, sending a sharp pain to my elbow. He fell against the newspaper stand. The stand creaked and moaned and a trash can fell over next to it.

The other man looked back as he fled. "Fucking asshole," he slurred.

I picked up my father by the shirt and landed another blow. And another.

The blood spurting from his nose woke me up and forced me to see his face more clearly.

He was just a drunk. Jesus.

NAKED

"We have to get out of here," I hissed at Cat. A muscle in my neck throbbed.

Cat stood still, gaping at the man, who struggled to his feet, one hand cradling his jaw.

I grabbed the brown bags of food and hurried her to the car. "Can't afford to get in trouble," I growled to myself.

Once we were driving on the roads again, I exhaled loudly, trying to get a grip on myself.

"*La force*. It is how you solve problems, no?" she said quietly.

"Please, Cat. Not now."

Studying my face, she noticed the cut on my jaw—the one I'd seen in the mirror this morning, scarring in the shape of the letter *S*. She lifted her hand to touch it, but I reached up and moved her hand back to her lap.

Silence sat between us.

"I can't help it, Cat. It's what I know."

"I begin to understand this about you."

J was studying the mismatched legs of *The Walking Man* when Jesse arrived the following night. He set a brown-paper bag on the bench and called to me, "Thank God you're still here. I thought maybe I'd come and you'd have disappeared." To himself, he muttered, "Everything's so surreal." Then he bowed his head. "Listen. I'm sorry about ruining things last night. I thought I was through with all that. My life is about as mixed up as yours. My temper caused trouble in the spring, and I almost lost my job."

"What happened?"

"I got in a fight outside the store. Someone called the cops. Shit. It was bad. Fuck . . . then at Stanford, the prof almost kicked me out for fighting this summer."

I was quiet. Hearing him tell his story reminded me of turning over a rock in a garden and finding a dark hidden world underneath.

"When I'm around you, I don't want you to have to worry about me," he said. "That's the most important thing. As if you haven't had enough trauma."

"It is time to find a different way."

He nervously rubbed at his chin. "Somehow . . . I have to."

I just listened, then pulled out the eating mat I was working on and set it on the picnic table. Weaving the threads in and out was comforting. If only everything could be put into order so easily.

The rhythm of the weaving seemed to calm both of us.

"I know I need to do something," he said. "I'm going to try to look at all this. I really am." His eyes had a sad tint to them. "We make quite a pair, don't we?"

I reached for his hand. "You and I together, it feels like one tidal wave and then another."

"So much drama. Things've got to settle down. I think they will." He looked over at the bag he had brought, still perched on the bench. "Will you eat dinner with me?" He sounded unsure.

I nodded, and he pulled out a transparent container. Inside, I studied the fish and rice in glistening black wrappings. It was a relief to focus on something outside of our problems.

"It's Japanese. Here're some chopsticks for you," he said. "We're having sushi."

"So interesting." My chopsticks crisscrossed pathetically when I tried to maneuver them, but he showed me how to hold the top one like a pencil. "That is a bit better," I said. "You know, I should be good at this—I am an artist, after all."

When I began stabbing the food, he took pity on me and fed me, amused by my struggles.

The fish was uncooked, except for the shrimp. The combination of tastes made me nearly chirp with pleasure. "Oh, I just remembered," I said between bites. "I need the poem 'Beauty' by Baudelaire."

"I could print it out for you at home," he said. "Why that one?"

"It is special. It inspired *Meditation*, the statue that is most dear to me. The one you touched."

I strained to hear what he said next. His voice was as soft as a lullaby. "Oh, Cat . . . sometimes I want you to take back everything you said and tell me a different story about how you got here."

"It does not have any sense to it, but we did find each other, no?"

"It's true," he said.

He fed me a piece of sushi with green paste on it. It stung my mouth in a pleasant way and made me cough.

"Maybe I'll use that statue in my performance piece," he said. "I only have a few more weeks before I've got to turn in my final draft."

"And then what happens, Jesse?" I sat motionless, waiting for an answer.

"And then Chapman. It turns out orientation is in the third week of August. A couple of weeks away."

The thought of his leaving made my vision blur. I held my temples and tried to focus on the twisted branch of a nearby tree, to steady myself.

Jesse scooted closer to me on the bench and held my bare shoulders. "We have to figure something out. I'm not leaving you here," he said. "You know that, right? We'll make a plan."

"I hope so," I said.

———◆———

My dreams turned to nightmares the evening after Jesse spoke of leaving for Chapman. Before that, my dream-images had been of the garden, of Jesse, or of Rodin, but nothing disturbing enough to wake me. Now the dark memories that had been submerged began to surface, like sea monsters showing their snouts above the waves.

That night, the agitated thrumming of my heart woke me. The nightmare was still present, although a bit faded: *I was standing with Rodin in his studio, asking him about marriage. The hesitation, the regret on his face was undeniable. I watched as my body stiffened, and I felt my heart tighten into a fist.*

The dream left me with a pulsing in my temples, and I couldn't return to sleep. An hour later, at four o'clock in the morning, I bathed in the fountain, hoping the cold water would wash the images away.

At midday, a young man and his father walked past me, with skin the color of the sculptures in late afternoon. Both were tall with short black hair.

"If you want to get in here . . . ." the father said.

"I don't know if I want to."

"If Stanford accepted you, you wouldn't go?"

"Too close to home."

Father and son settled their long legs under the picnic table next to *Caryatid with Stone*. They bit into their sandwiches in unison.

"I guess I can understand that," said the father, shaking his head. "How far away is far enough?"

Far away. The words drummed in my head all day as I sketched. He would be far away from me . . . if we could not find a plan.

"*So*, you don't have long for this grocery world, huh, Jesse?" Jim said.

We were out back in the sun, Jim with sunglasses, me squinting. The whapping as we piled the cardboard boxes on top of each other was satisfying in its own way.

"Yeah, you're gonna be on your own, bro. Sorry about that. Hey, what did Terry say?"

"Fuck." Jim spit on the ground. "He said he couldn't think of one reason to give me a raise or a recommendation to move to another store in a different position. That's the only way to move up, it turns out."

"What a bastard."

"The whole thing is so grim, I'm thinking of taking a class or two at community college."

"Seriously? That'd be great."

"Yeah, something practical, like business—nothing crazy like acting." Jim winked at me.

"Thanks for the vote of confidence."

"No, really, I think you'll make it, dude. And I'll say I knew you when."

"Ha! Listen, Jim, I got one last thing to toss around with you."

"Yeah, right. You'll be texting me your problems from college. Wise as I am."

"Shut up for a minute and just tell me I'm not nuts."

"Specifically, how aren't you nuts?"

"I'm thinking Cat has to come with me, somehow."

"Well, sure, she should come with you. If you're that serious about her."

"But she doesn't have any money. She's . . . homeless. She . . . ." I couldn't tell him everything.

"What? So I was right?" Jim interrupted my thoughts.

"Yeah."

"Bro, what're you gonna do? Hide her in your suitcase? Better leave some breathing holes."

"Shut the fuck up. How could I bring her? Really."

"Use your brains, dude. You got 'em, use 'em. Ya know, I'm gonna miss hearing about your fucked-up life when you leave. I think."

"Right." I laughed half-heartedly and stomped on a box.

"Don't worry about Cat. You'll think of something, Jesse."

"Cat, I've been thinking nonstop about us. And I've got an idea."
She sighed and bit at her lip. I sat down with her as she slipped her pencil into the wire binding of her sketchpad and looked away from her drawing of *The Gates of Hell*.

My hands braced either side of her face. "You should see your expression. I'm going to make you smile if it kills me."

"What is your idea? Make me smile."

"You'll come with me. We'll get you into art classes, and you'll build a portfolio. We'll get you a scholarship once—"

"I love classes, but—"

"But what? It's going to be raining in late fall, cold during the day and night. You're crazy if you think I'll let you freeze your butt off out here." I pulled her toward me and made our bodies sway back and forth, trying to pull a laugh out of her.

She arched back and looked at me. "And what of money? How will I pay for the classes? For food? Where will I live?"

"I'm figuring it all out. I'm looking up grants online. We'll make it work." I brushed a spider off my forearm.

"I do not understand what you said, but—"

"Cat, I know you're worried. I won't leave you. I won't." I sat on a bench and pulled her by the hips until she was in front of me. "It's going to take you trusting me. Can you do that?" I drew her closer, between my legs. "I've never been this certain of anything, and I refuse to let you live here much longer."

She smiled, squeezed my shoulders, and kissed me.

"That's better," I said. "And here's something else to make you smile."

Out of my pack, I pulled a grass-green summer dress with a pattern of yellow flowers on it. I held it up. The shop owner said she liked the curved neckline and the small ruffles on the shoulders.

"This vintage store was having a closing sale, and I couldn't help but bring you this. Do you like it?"

Cat crushed the fabric in her hands and pressed it against her body to see how it would look.

"How wonderful, Jesse. You picked this out yourself?"

"Try it on in my car," I said.

She nearly danced to the car, and came back with the dress over her tights.

"I should go back and buy the whole rack for you. You look gorgeous."

"Thank you," she said, feeling the material from her hips to her legs.

I twirled her to the right and then to the left, and picked her up off the ground. When I set her down again, she noticed the books I'd piled on the bench. "You have to work, no?"

"I guess so," I sighed.

Among the books, *Inferno* caught her attention. "Dante?" she asked.

"Yeah, that's the direction I'm going. I really need to get a chunk of this out of the way tonight. Have to turn in my idea for the performance piece."

"What subject did you choose?"

"It's about rage, violence. I can't see doing anything else."

She slid off the bench and slipped her hoodie over the dress, suddenly quieter, inside herself. I shuffled through the books, sorry I'd broken the mood, and started reading Dante's poetry.

*J*esse's words opened the door to uninvited memories. I sat down on the bench with him and closed my eyes. Clear images surfaced of my last day with Rodin: *Taking the sketches of the Balzac statue from Rodin and setting them on a worktable. Facing him and holding his hands, proposing marriage to him. Rodin silent, his eyelids lowered, his color pale. Then saying that he wanted to be with me, but he couldn't marry me, that he couldn't leave Rose, as he had promised. Turning my back to him. My body shuddering when his hand touched my shoulder for the very last time. The clatter of my high-heeled boots on the cobblestones outside the studio, resentment filling my heart and billowing like a wind-whipped fire. Furious at him, and at me. For being such a fool.*

My hands covered my chest, and I gasped.

"Cat, what's wrong?" Jesse glanced up from his computer. I was so buried in the past, I was almost shocked to see him and could not speak for a full minute. When he reached for me, I motioned him back.

"I have nightmares, flashes of remembering," I said.

"What nightmares?" From his eyes, he seemed to want to hear and not to hear. "What happened to you?"

I held tightly to my upper arms, embracing myself. I did not know what to say at first, but then I put words to my memories. "Rodin did not choose me. He chose the woman he lived with. Rose. He betrayed a promise, even though our lives were attached in so many different ways. Even though I was his muse. After that, I walked down a very dark path." My temples ached, and I pressed against them with the heels of my hands. "Some of the past, I still cannot remember completely. I do not dare to. Not yet."

As Jesse's eyes searched mine, the crease between his brows deepened. Then he kissed the middle of my forehead.

"Do not worry." I said, pointing to his books. "You should work now."

He pulled some work pages from his pack, and a folded sheet of paper dropped to the ground.

"That poem you wanted," he said, handing it to me.

Unfolding the rumpled page, I found the poem that had inspired *Meditation*. Drawn to the first stanza, I reread it several times.

BEAUTY
by Charles Baudelaire

I am as lovely as a dream in stone,
And this my heart where each finds death in turn,
Inspires the poet with a love as lone
As clay eternal and as taciturn.

So, for Rodin, the *Meditation* statue was a beautiful dream in stone, that he loved, that inspired him. But he could never truly communicate with the bronze woman he had sculpted. I shivered, though the air was not cold. Was this what he thought of me? Perhaps it was. I tucked the poem into my sketchpad.

Turning to a fresh page, I smoothed it out for some time with my fingertips, lost in thought. Then I began a drawing of a new version of *Meditation*—a woman meditating on a bench. As I sketched, Jesse typed.

*C*at had revealed more than ever, and it was doing a number on my mind. Damn. I needed to hold on until I could take her somewhere she could get help.

I opened my computer, hoping to be able to focus. It was time to make some decisions about my piece.

August 6
Jesse Lucas
Research/Topic exploration for performance piece

The performance piece is supposed be personal. I'm thinking anger/rage has got to be my big concept. I keep groping for something safer, but every time I look at *The Gates of Hell*, it's confirmed. With Rodin's sculptures as a buffer, maybe I can make myself look at my own stuff—though how deeply, I don't know yet.

The facts: *The Gates of Hell* took twenty years to complete (1880–1900)—what a massive project. In the beginning, Camille posed for some of the figures and probably created some in clay. By the time the gates were finished, Camille had a set of sculptures in marble and bronze, and Rodin was world famous.

The Thinker on *The Gates of Hell* was originally supposed to be the author Dante—Rodin thought he was going to base *The Gates* on Dante's *Inferno*. I can see how the verses about violence fit the suffering in the figures on *The Gates*. And inside me. They tell the story of me . . . and D. There's even one passage about being "greedy for revenge." Fuck, do I know that one.

Rodin didn't stick with illustrating the stories in Dante's *Inferno*, because he started to think that hell comes from inside, that men and women are tormented by their passions that can never be satisfied. I would bet Rodin was talking about his passion for Camille.

And in my case? Shit. My passion/torment is all about anger, blame, revenge—the whole package. I think wrath was one of Dante's seven deadly sins, but anyone would feel it in my situation. D works himself up and takes it out on me, over and over. In my mind, I fight back and beat him up until he can't move or speak. Or do one more thing to me.

The Gates of Hell make so much sense now—they've got to be the center of my piece. But I'll use the other statues, too. Maybe drape them in red. Maybe use blindfolds. I wish I could do it in the daytime and get random reactions, but Stanford would never give permission, not in such a short time anyway. It'll have to be night. I'm ready to pin this thing down. Finally.

I exhaled to expel some of the energy inside me. So much was coming together, and so much was whirling out of control. The whole idea that Cat believed her spirit was inside the statue, the things she told me about Rodin. It was almost too much to fucking think about—it was so bizarre.

I sat motionless, focused internally, until I forced myself to shake out my hands, unkink my neck, and stretch my legs. Cat looked up at me and moistened her pencil on the tip of her tongue.

"Cat, it seems to me that Rodin was totally obsessed with Camille, tormented by his passion for her."

"His passion for *me*, yes." Her voice had a gentleness to it. "I know this is strange for you, but it is in the past. I do not love Rodin now. I love you, Jesse, and our love is not strange, only the circumstance."

I touched her hand. Would I go crazy along with her by not challenging what she said, by just listening? Or had I already lost my mind?

She was disturbingly convincing—if I let in her story even for a minute, everything somehow shifted into place in a very surreal way. I had to admit it, even though I tried to push it away.

To keep a grip on sanity, I told myself that Cat and I were the only ones in the garden that night because we were meant to know each other, to love each other, whether she was mad or not. It was beyond fucking coincidence. Somehow, that felt real without messing with my head.

I ran my fingers over the computer keys to get back to some sort of reality, something I could touch. "I think I'm getting somewhere in my performance piece."

"Tell me about it."

"Well, Rodin was inspired by Dante when he sketched the sections of *The Gates of Hell*, right? So, I'm finding all these quotes from Dante that refer to violence and wrath. Revenge is in there, too."

"That is you . . . your fa—"

"Please, Cat. I'm not ready to get into that—"

"When will you be ready? When you blame him for everything that goes wrong with you—"

"Cat—"

"—your resentment destroys you."

"Stop. I really can't go there right now."

She laid her pencil in the gravel and stood next to *Caryatid with Urn*, holding onto the thick leg of the statue. "I am sorry, Jesse. Just go step by step. It is my dark dreams. They make me irritable."

"Cat, you shouldn't be sleeping facing *The Gates of Hell*." I laughed softly. "Did you ever think of that? It's got to be making it worse for you."

"If you knew how I feel, you would not laugh."

"You know I'm just trying to help. These statues you're bedding down next to—*Meditation, Martyr, The Three Shades*—they're all embedded in the gates. No pun intended," I said. "Why sleep at the Gates of Hell if you don't have to?"

That made her smile. "Maybe I will move there, to that bench." She pointed to the section of the garden beyond the row of trees.

When it was time for me to go home that night, she held onto me a little longer than normal. I could tell she was thinking about me leaving for Chapman, for good. What she didn't realize was how stubborn I could be about what I wanted.

*J*n order to ward off the nightmares, I gathered wildflowers and fresh grasses and made an altar in front of the new bench. I meditated before I lay down, and even placed a flower on my tongue.

But in the middle of the night, I woke with a start and sat straight up on the hard bench. Slowly, I pieced together the nightmare: *I was clutching my shawl around me and telling Rodin's messenger, "I have not left my studio for months. Why would I want to attend any events with Rodin, even for business? Tell him I am taking full charge of my own affairs now, my sculpting and my exhibitions. I do not need his help. I do not want it." Then I was shutting the studio door, shutting myself away from the outside world, into an inner world of dark, vengeful thoughts toward Rodin. He had used me. But never again!*

I rubbed my face to completely wake myself from the nightmare and surveyed the garden. I was far from the main body of sculptures. Sleeping away from them obviously had not helped. I struggled to fall back to sleep and could not. But during the day, I found myself napping in a sitting position to replenish my energy.

When Jesse arrived, he had a large roll of brown paper tucked under his arm.

"Cat! I'm finally here. So much is unraveling, and you're the only one who'd understand."

He unrolled the paper in front of my new bench, on a large circle of gravel. The heads of two of *The Burghers of Calais* peered down at us from their pedestals. On the paper, he had drawn the ensemble of garden statues in a sketchy way. Each statue had a splotch of red painted on its face.

"I'm calling my performance piece *Masquerage*," he said. "I'm trying to create something from my anger, like you said to."

"*Mon dieu*, Jesse. You really listened to me?"

"Occasionally, I actually do listen," he joked.

"What will you do in your piece?"

"I'll read verses from Dante, for sure."

"Hmm. And the red color?" I pointed to his drawing.

"I'm going to blindfold some of the statues."

"On the eyes?"

"Some eyes, gags on some mouths."

"Tell me more about it."

"And then I'll read more passages from Dante and remove the cloths. And underneath . . . ."

"*Oui*, underneath?"

"Honestly, I don't know yet. I'm just figuring it out. Will you help me? We can do some improvising as we go along."

"Of course." I pinched at my neck, which felt tight and knotted.

"If you're up for it, we'll film tomorrow night." Jesse reached over and rubbed the muscles of my neck.

"Night is not safe," I said. "You must wait until after four o'clock in the morning."

"Why?"

"The police often pass by at that time. I know."

"Hmm. Four o'clock won't leave me much of an audience. That could be a problem. Course, I guess you'd be the audience. Is that okay with you? You'd be a participating audience, though, because I need you to film. My prof might not approve, but I've just got to do the best I can. Maybe the film itself will be more important to the piece than he wants it to be."

Rolling my neck in a circle, I yawned. "I will help you. But I must rest a bit now, Jesse. I still do not sleep well."

"Sure. Go ahead."

I sat on my new bench, and he sat beside me. When I curled up next to him, nestling under his arm, I felt a warmth traveling between us. He must have felt it too, for he began nuzzling my neck and kissing my mouth and the tops of my breasts. After I assented, he massaged me on top of my clothes, all over my body, including my inner thighs and buttocks. Inside me, a heat was building. I sat up and kissed him deeply, explored his chest with my fingers, sure I could feel his heartbeat, and then moved down to his legs, following the length of the muscles in his strong thighs. He boosted me onto his lap, and I let him find my breasts inside my top and pinch my nipples, but when he began to reach into my tights, I gently removed his hand.

"Not now," I said. "It feels so good. But not now."

"Mmm, it feels more than good. It's not easy to stop," he said. He kissed me quickly, then placed his arms under my legs and lifted me off of him. Standing, he clasped his hands, stretched his arms upward, and groaned.

"I'll let you really get some sleep now," he said, with a grin. "I need to get everything ready anyway. Download the music and all that. Download myself somehow," he laughed. "I've got plenty to do. And I won't wake you when I leave."

When he settled on a bench nearby and disappeared into his work, fatigue overwhelmed me. Falling into a troubled sleep, the nightmares seeped their way in again: *My studio was cramped and crowded with sculptures in different stages. In the dark, people were climbing in the windows, throwing billowing white sheets over my plaster statues, and carrying them off. I tried to wrench my sculptures from their arms, but they kicked at my legs and marched out the front door, laughing at me. "I know who sent you," I screamed after them. "Rodin sent you! He is a thief! He always has been!"*

My dream-screeches startled me awake. I was alone. I wondered about the dream, if it could possibly be true. I sat still, letting the images settle in my mind. Could I bear to remember all of what happened to me? I remained upright on the bench, eyes wide open, afraid to dream again.

———— ◆ ————

Jesse brought roasted chicken and potatoes with parsley for dinner the following night. My stomach full of warm food, I felt my energy returning.

"Tonight's the night," he said. He seemed to be vibrating with anticipation. "I borrowed a friend's camera. Have to return it tomorrow."

I helped him unload the equipment from his car. Out of his pack, he pulled a dozen blood-red cloths. Inside a bag made of a coarse blue fabric were white candles, candleholders, and dark masks. I could scarcely look at the masks.

"They remind me of my nightmares. Last night . . . ."

"What happened?"

"I . . . I dreamed that Rodin stole my sculptures."

"Do you think he really did?" Jesse took my hands in his. His eyes had a look of sadness, as they often did when I spoke of Rodin.

"All I know is my dream. It seemed so vivid, so real. I dread to go to sleep again, but I must rest before we begin. Wake me when it is time."

We watched the moon, and the summer planet Jupiter, until I fell into a fitful sleep on the new bench. The bell tower rang four times in the background of my dream when I felt Jesse's touch on my shoulder. "It's time," he said.

It was hard to extract myself from my nightmare: *Rodin had sent an older woman in a white apron to my studio. The woman set out a cup of steaming tea and slipped a thick liquid into it, unaware that I was watching her from a doorway. I stomped into the room and confronted the woman, shouting in her face, "I see what you are doing. Rodin is trying to poison me now!" In one movement, I grasped the cup and dashed it to the floor, where it shattered into tiny white pieces, jagged and irregular.*

Upon waking, I sat as still as a statue, reflecting on what I had seen. Then I closed my eyes and watched the dream-memory unfold again. But this time I saw it from a distance—from the vast distance between the present and the past: *This time, I recognized that the woman was simply a housekeeper who had come to help me straighten my disheveled studio. I had observed the woman doing the same at Rodin's quarters. Inspecting the liquid more closely, I recognized its golden color and smelled its honeysuckle scent. It was thick honey, fresh from the market. Not poison at all.*

I opened my eyes slowly so as not to lose this knowledge about the past. A chill of excitement raised bumps on my arms. Then I patted my face and my limbs, to wake up to the present, with Jesse.

I scanned the garden. On top of each of the ground lights, he had placed a candle. The light flickering over the statues was constantly changing.

"Are you ready, Cat? You okay to go?" he asked. "I just want to show you how to use the camera. It's easy. You look in here. This zooms in and out for close-ups, and this is On and Off." He carefully settled the camera on a bench.

The computer buzzed to life under his fingers, and soon, discordant music blared from its shell. I could not clearly understand the words of the male singer. His voice was harsh.

"That's 'Search and Destroy.' It's Iggy and the Stooges. I relate," he said. "Can you help me put these blindfolds on the statues?"

Using a three-legged stool he had brought, he fastened the red blindfolds around the taller statues. I tied the cloths around the eyes of the *Caryatids*, the mouth of *Martyr*, the eyes of *Meditation*. *Adam* was blindfolded, and *Eve* was gagged in front of *The Gates of Hell*.

"Can I cover your mouth, too, Cat? Would that be okay? Or would it freak you out?"

I gave my consent and felt the cotton cloth binding my lips, as Jesse's fingers tied it behind me and pulled gently at the strands of hair that were tangled in the gag.

"If you're okay with it, it might be good if you moved through the statues now, maybe ending at *The Gates of Hell*," he said.

I smoothed out my new dress, and in the eerie light, I started at *Orpheus* and flitted through the garden, alternating between the dark of the night and the light from the candles below. I was hardly aware of Jesse making a film of me, as I moved from statue to statue, acknowledging each one as I peered from behind it or brushed in front of it. I was deeply aware that I had once been as silent and still as they were, inside *Meditation*. My breath dampened the red cloth over my mouth, and I could hear my own rough breathing, as a dark, anxious feeling began to seep into my body.

When I came to the gates, I removed my gag and placed my palm on my chest, trying to calm myself. Jesse handed me the camera and sat down, cross-legged. Once my fingers were securely around the camera strap, he instructed me. "After you find me in the lens, move the camera around—only show parts of my face, or half my face. It should look unbalanced. Some should be so close up, you can't tell what part of my body you're filming."

As I filmed, Jesse recited Dante in a low voice. I was chilled by his words.

The river of blood, within which boiling is . . . .

In the camera's window, I found his hands and parts of his body—the curve of his neck, the shape of his bent leg—then moved to his face, framing only his mouth, only his eyes, only a piece of his profile.

. . . Whoe'er by violence doth injure others.

Jesse pointed at *The Gates* and I moved the camera down the left side and then the right, filming *The Thinker* and showing close-ups of the figures in agony—*Ugolino, Paolo and Francesca, The Three Shades*. He recited quotes from Dante, about violence and revenge, his voice deep and haunting.

. . . And there are those whom injury seems to chafe,
So that it makes them greedy for revenge.

The words knocked forcefully at the door of my own vengefulness and refused to leave.

"Let's unmask them now," Jesse said, handing me scissors. "I'll film you."

I heard moans and odd squeaks coming from my mouth as I cut the cloth from each statue, while Jesse followed with the camera, placing the camera's eye very close to the expressions Rodin had sculpted. I shivered to see the eyes and mouths underneath—the agony, despair, sorrow.

"This is very difficult, Jesse." My voice broke. "I am trying hard not to cry, or scream."

"Can you keep going?" His voice was so husky, I almost did not recognize it.

"I think it helps me," I said.

I had the camera again. Hunched over his computer, Jesse set up another song.

"This is Iggy Pop," he said. "It's called 'Mask.'" The voice of a man shouted his pain.

His back still turned, Jesse dug into the duffel bag. When he faced me, he was wearing many layers of masks, and over them, a red cloth bound his mouth. I led him to the center of the garden, next to a candle that lit his face when he sat down behind it. I turned on the camera again. The Iggy Pop song filled the air as Jesse removed the red cloth. Underneath was a monster mask with a contorted grimace. He pulled it off quickly to reveal a snarling skull. Under that was a mangled face half melted away, and under that a black-eyed zombie, its mouth a black hole. This last mask, he left on.

In his hand, he held something silver. A knife.

As I watched, he plunged the knife into the gravel, full force, over and over, yelling and roaring, "I hate you. Motherfucker. Prick," as the music blasted over his voice, the singer chanting words of pain.

I hid behind the camera, filming, my own feelings reverberating with the tones in his voice and the movement of the knife. It seemed as if he would never stop. Then I screamed inside, and out loud—unable to distinguish between my outer and inner voices, between my voice and Jesse's, between my emerging memories of the past and the cacophony around me. Without warning, Jesse let go of the knife and pulled off the zombie mask. Under it was his own face—spent, slack, eyes looking inward.

I scanned his face with the camera as he recited Dante, his voice hoarse now.

Hence thou mayst comprehend that love must be
The seed within yourselves of every virtue.

"Revolution," he whispered at the end, and I felt tears on my cheeks, for him and for me.

He sat still for what seemed like five minutes. When he slowly rose to his feet, he appeared to be larger than life-size, and his brown eyes looked clear. I turned off the camera and set it on the bench. He came toward me, and then he was lifting me, carrying me to the area behind the benches and gently setting me down on the dark grass that was now damp.

"Cat," he said, in a low voice. "You gave me the guts to feel all that. It was fucking me up, eating at me like acid." His hands touched either side of my face. "It's just a start, but I feel different already." He lay back on the grass and pulled me down next to him. Then he was lying on top of me, his elbows on either side of my head. "I could feel us both going through it."

"*Oui*," I stretched my arms above my head. "Together."

We rolled and rolled on the grass. We growled and laughed and kissed each other over and over. He bit at my neck.

"You have become a vampire now?" I laughed.

My hands wove through the tufts of his hair and pulled on them. His hands explored my face, my neck, each breast, inside my dress. Beneath his shirt, I ran my hands over the muscles of his chest. His hand stroked each of my thighs under my tights, and even between my legs where my heart seemed to be beating. Jesse and I were not just sculptors this time. My fingers felt his hips, his pelvis. He placed my hand on the bulge in his pants.

"Jesse," I murmured, barely remembering how to form words, "I am not ready."

"I know, I know. Slowly," he said. He moved his hand to my forehead and stroked my hair. His hand smelled of me.

"Thank you." I kissed his mouth. I could trust him. I could be close to him. He was safe.

*T*he next night, everyone in class was buzzing. Most of us had finished our performance pieces or were editing the films we'd made of them.

"I should have cut my real hair," Lisa said, as she slid in a seat beside me. "My piece is kind of lame."

"I'm sure it's fine."

"Back to your garden visits, huh?"

"Yeah, you been following me?" I teased.

"No, just noticed where you headed."

"Right."

She smiled. "You can't stop my fantasies, you know."

That made me laugh.

We spent most of the class checking in individually with Marc Stein. He actually liked my film, but wished I'd had more of an audience.

After class, I made my way over to Tito.

"What do ya want, psycho?"

"Tito, I'm sorry. I just got fucked up over a girl."

He stared at me like I was nuts to even talk to him.

"Jesus, man. You were so fucked, I thought you were kidding, or beyond wasted, or high on meth, or . . . ."

"Sorry, man."

He chucked me on the arm and laughed. "I've seen guys who had it much worse than you. Just don't go off on me again."

"For sure."

"Hey, before I forget, give me your number in case I'm ever in L.A. Maybe I could crash at your place."

"Anytime."

I practically skipped to the garden. But when I saw Cat on her bench, I remembered filming her, and a twinge of anxiety pushed the class from my mind. I slid in beside her and clasped her hands in mine. Tried to keep my voice calm. "Hey, Cat. How're you doing?"

"I am tired from our filming, but happy it is done."

"I've really got to talk to you about something."

"What is it?"

"The strangest damn thing . . . in the film . . . why don't you show up? Were you ducking away from the camera?"

"What are you saying?"

"When you were dancing through the statues, you look like . . . a ghost, or a shape made of tiny lights."

"Oh, no." Her hands covered her mouth.

"It scared me. What does it mean?"

"I am afraid it . . . it perhaps means I am changing back."

"Dammit, Cat. No! It's got to be something else." I fumbled for words. "It's got to be because you aren't like everyone else. But you're not a ghost." Panic rose like a swelling river in my chest.

"I am not. Yet in this incarnation, Jesse, I never know how long I have."

"Nobody knows how long they have. Cat, you're really freaking me out. I've never let myself get so close to anyone before. I'm not losing you no matter what this means." I grabbed her hands.

"I have never been so close, too."

"Forget the fucking film." I touched her cheek. "What we've got is stronger than some dumb camera or some crazy phenomenon. Let's focus on us leaving. Once you're out of here, you'll be more grounded. Everything'll be more stable."

"Perhaps it is true."

"After you have a portfolio, you can apply for a college scholarship. Everyone will see that you're gifted."

"But, tell me the truth, where would I live?"

I stroked her hair and tucked it behind her shoulders. "You'll stay in my room at school till we find something else. Or maybe in a room at an art collective—I saw some ads about that. I've got a job in food service. It's perfect. Just think about it. It'll work out."

"I am always thinking about it, Jesse."

We held each other, our faces nestled in each other's necks.

"I love you, Cat."

"I love you, Jesse Lucas."

———◆———

I lay on my bed for a long time, picturing both of us in Los Angeles. Then I got up, spell-checked my paper, took out a few references to Dad, and printed out the pages so far. Mom had left me an envelope with a hundred-dollar bill in it. The note said, *Get what you need for your room at Chapman. Just sold my quilt. Love, Mom.*

As the printer shuffled and groaned, I heard the door opening and twisted in my chair to see what was up.

In stepped Dad.

"You took money out of your account again." He stayed by the door.

"I have things I need to buy."

"You have things you need to buy," he mimicked and stepped a foot closer. "Are you saying you don't appreciate your free room and board?"

I slipped my printed pages into my pack to protect them and stood up.

He strode across the room until he was facing me, a foot and a half away.

"You listening to me?" he asked. "Are ya?"

He threw a right to my jaw.

I saw it coming and raised my forearm to block it. I felt the whack on my arm, but my face was untouched. Dad's mouth opened in surprise.

Energy surged through me, and I grabbed him in a bear hug, pinning his arms to his sides.

"It's over, Dad. This shit you've got going isn't about me." With all my strength, I walked him backwards toward the door. "It never has been."

He kicked at me, but I didn't let go. I was a lot bulkier than he was. Had been for a long time.

"Who the fuck do you think you are?" he yelled, finally bucking himself out of my grasp. "Don't you dare disrespect me like that! Get out of my house!"

He kept on yelling, but he didn't put up his fists.

My forehead was damp with sweat. "That's what you want?"

"Get your ass out. Now!"

"Goodbye then, Dad."

"I won't pay one fucking cent for college." He headed for the door.

"I've got my own loans."

"Someday you'll see you threw everything away. Dig your own grave, Jesse."

The door slammed shut. It was quiet, but the air was vibrating around me.

I threw clothes, books, and stuff from the bathroom into two big duffle bags Mom had given me for college. I was breathing as heavily as if I'd just sprinted a half mile.

I loaded the car in three trips, then came back in for the last time. Mom was sitting upright on the couch, tearing up. I leaned down and kissed her on the head.

"I'll write you, Mom. I'll find a way to see you." She held my hand, then let it go.

It didn't take me long to get to the garden. The screech of my brakes made Cat look up. I parked haphazardly in front of *The Three Shades*, jumped out, slammed the door, and ran to her.

I could hardly catch my breath. My body began shaking as soon as I dropped down onto the bench beside her.

"I did it," I said. "I never could've done it before I met you. Never. I had no idea how important it was."

She touched my leg and set down her drawing.

"Let's walk. I can't sit still," I said. As we headed down the road I squeezed her hand, hard. It took me a minute to realize she was wiggling her fingers to get me to loosen my hold. "I was printing my paper last night. Dad came home late from work—he was steaming, looking for a target. Something set him off at the station. He was going off on me, really in my face. I stood there opposite him . . . ."

"What happened?"

"He raised his arms to pummel me, threw a punch . . . ."

"And . . . ?"

"I blocked him. Stood up to him. He starts yelling at me, then kicks me out. I packed and walked out of that house for good. I can't spend my life battling him, hating him. I've got too much I want to do."

"Your eyes, they are still deep," she said, "but they look brighter, lighter in color. Is this possible?"

I smiled at her. Then I laughed a little. "I'm homeless now, too."

"Where will you live?"

"In my car, I guess."

We headed back toward the garden. In the distance, I could see *The Gates of Hell*.

"What about your mother, Jesse?"

"I'll definitely e-mail her, and figure out how to visit her."

I glanced around the garden. "I guess I'll be sleeping here. But not tonight. I might just drive around."

She nodded. "Do whatever it is you need to do."

"You were right, Cat."

"About what?"

"It wasn't something I could figure out in my head, this rage thing. I had to feel all of it. Last night, when we were filming, I could feel how it was tearing me down, holding me hostage."

"I understand." She was quiet, then, "It happened with me, too. I began to see my own anger from my past life, from a different view."

"I'm glad," I said, stepping closer, "because I owe you, Cat." We wrapped our arms around each other's waists, until every part of our bodies was touching.

"We are melded together as if we are made of fresh clay," she said.

"You know, you're much more than a muse to me."

She smiled. And she understood when I had to leave, be alone, have time for it all to settle in. I drove around for hours, in the foothills behind the campus. I returned to Cat at four in the morning, but I hardly said a word.

"You are like a sea snail in its shell," she said.

Still I couldn't say anything.

When we were huddled on the bench, I finally spoke, "Underneath . . . ."

"What?"

"Underneath is sadness . . . I know it for sure now."

"Under the anger?"

"Yeah . . . I want a dad."

I couldn't keep my body from shaking. She held me, and I hugged her back.

We stayed like that, wafting in and out of sleep, until the sun rose and the clock chimed seven times in the distance.

I carefully untangled my body from hers. "I've got to go to work. I'll see you tonight, Cat."

———◦◦———

I walked slowly toward her when I returned that night and cupped her shoulders, which were cool to the touch.

"Are you committed to me?" I studied her face. "Because I'm committed to you, Cat."

"*Oui*," she said. "I am committed to you, Jesse." Her hands moved to my hips. "It was fate, no? It brought us together, and now, both of us feel more whole."

As I drew her to me, we looked over to my car at the same time and smiled. With urgency, and a great deal of shuffling of papers and slapping of books into piles, we moved my belongings to the trunk and front seat of the car. Then we climbed into the back seat. I carefully laid her down, spread her legs, and lay on top of her. She wrapped her legs around me. When we kissed, I thought of *The Kiss*—I felt like we inspired it.

I held her head in my hands and kissed her with my whole mouth. It was like she was inside me and I was inside her. I gently unzipped her skirt, pulled it down her legs. She unbuttoned my shirt. We laughed because there was so little room to move. She opened the squeaky door, and we climbed out into the night and became naked, naked as the statues. But more beautiful. Life-size. Real. Committed.

In the back seat again, we intertwined every limb that could be intertwined. My lips traveled her body, from her forehead to her lips to her throat. Her breasts, her belly, between her legs where she was wet and slick, her thighs, her toes. With her warm lips and tongue, she kissed my cheeks and licked my ears, my chest. And lower . . . my stomach muscles . . . and lower . . . my penis. Her soft mouth was around me. I groaned as I reached on the floor where I'd dropped a condom, and rolled it on.

I was on top of her again and then I pushed inside of her, filling her. I felt like we were made of molten metal that burst into form. And then we cooled and slept, bound together like two figures from a sculpture.

*A*t three in the morning, according to the clock tower, I woke from my dreams. I studied his face and brushed my lips across his cheek. He was so beautiful. When I slipped out of his grasp, he was deep in sleep and didn't seem to know I had left.

After dressing by the car, I walked to my bench and lay on the familiar wood slats, to have my nightmare-memories alone. And they came, as they always did now, when I fell into sleep: *My last exhibition. My large sculptures were displayed in a Paris gallery, on pedestals, on the floor. I strode among them, silent at first, a fury building inside me. Then I was waving my arms and shouting above the polite conversation, "Rodin uses me. He steals my ideas. He is a scoundrel." The patrons, even my brother, stared wide-eyed, mouths twisted in shock. But I stomped my feet and would not, could not stop my ranting, even when my brother caught up with me, grasped my arm, and begged me to.*

When I awoke, I sat very still, the images still clear. I had so much talent and passion, but no peace. I was filled with blame. I blamed Rodin for trying to possess me, for taking too much inspiration from my work, for choosing Rose, not me. Across the chasm between the present and the past, I wanted to reach out to my past self. I wanted to embrace her, reassure her, comfort her. But my past self was not ready to give up the resentment. I had to leave her be.

A few hours later, I watched the sun rise behind the trees in the field and heard the familiar squeak of Jesse's car door opening. From a distance, I observed him wandering through the field and then crossing the road, searching for me. In his hand he held a bouquet of wildflowers. "I have to leave for the grocery store, but these are for you, until I see you tonight."

I tucked a flower into my hair, then kissed his cheeks, his mouth. "Thank you, thank you." My heart felt as if it were expanding beyond the bounds of my body.

———•◆•———

That night, when I saw him approaching, his pack hanging from one hand, I ran to him and hugged him. He lifted me easily off the ground. "Cat, I was thinking about you all day."

"You were inside my thoughts, too. I thought of you and laughed out loud." I stepped onto his toes and he walked me around in a circle.

"You were laughing at me?" He pretended to be angry.

"I laughed to think I was so lucky."

He studied my face. "I can't believe how beautiful you are. I love the untamable look in your eyes."

I kissed his cheeks, and he danced me around the perimeter of *The Three Shades* and around *Martyr*. His hand on my upper back, he dipped me down so far, I screamed and laughed. "Rascal," I shouted.

After I stepped off his feet, I tried to hand him his pack but strained to lift it even a centimeter off the ground. "What do you have inside? A slab of marble?"

"I'm almost finished with my paper," he said. "But there's so much to learn about Camille . . . ." His voice was a whisper. "About what happened to you. It's no wonder your dreams are so heavy."

"*Oui.* My life was very sad in the end." My throat was filling with tears. "Just do the work you need to do, Jesse."

"Are you okay?"

"I am better than in a very long time."

On his bench, Jesse spread out books on either side of him, and I glanced at the covers: me in a long striped dress, Rodin and I at a café, sculptures we had each created about our love affair.

I turned away, retrieved my sketchpads from under my bench, and set them on my lap. Starting at the beginning of the first pad, I turned the pages slowly. Each revealed a piece of my history with Jesse. On the first empty page, I started a preliminary drawing of two lovers, Jesse and me. I quickly sketched the movement of the two figures, the man kneeling, kissing the woman below her breasts, the woman's body bent slightly backward. On the facing page, I drew it again, with more specific, more confident strokes, and began rendering the shadows. I sensed it was very much like a sculpture I had created a lifetime ago.

Memories began drifting in, and I found my eyes closing to capture them: *I was in my studio, feeding the cats in a tiny bedroom next to my workspace. The lights were off. The pum pum of Jesse's fingers on the keys sounded like the rain on my studio roof . . . .*

*I*t was time to look head on at what happened to Camille, to Cat, in the last part of her life. I'd kept my distance from it as long as I could. It was going to be even harder to look at now that I was starting to piece things together. Now that I saw that something beyond logic must have happened to Cat, for her to be here with me. Nothing made sense, and everything made some sort of crazyass sense. But I was somehow beginning to accept it on some level—as wild as it all was.

August 11
Jesse Lucas
Research

Camille asked Rodin to marry her around 1893. When Rodin couldn't get himself to leave Rose, Camille split from him, found her own studio, and sculpted alone. Rodin was so miserable he could hardly work on the Balzac statue. So why didn't he marry her? Did he know he couldn't live with her, even though he loved her? Did he think she was unbalanced? Or did he know all along that he wouldn't leave Rose, because she took care of him so well?

    After their breakup, Camille's sculptures were strong: *The Gossipers* (speaks for itself), *Clotho* (the Fate in mythology who spun the thread of life), and *Maturity* (the love triangle between Rodin, Camille, and Rose). Mostly through letters, she still communicated with Rodin, asking his advice about finances, commenting on his Balzac statue. But then she fell into poverty, and called off business meetings with him and art dealers. At that point, she was pretty damned isolated, didn't leave her studio for months.

Gradually, but steadily, she let her appearance go—dressed in old baggy clothes, stopped bathing. Her studio apartment was filled with cobwebs and a dozen cats. Finally, she lost touch with reality/her creativity/herself.

She thought Rodin was jealous of her talent as a sculptor, even though he helped her get into the Paris Salon, introduced her to art critics, wanted her to use his connections even after they split. She was convinced he was copying/stealing her ideas to increase his fortune, while she was destitute.

When her brother Paul came to visit, he found her disheveled and raging about housekeepers, Rodin's models, and art people drugging her and damaging her sculptures. And she was dead sure that all of them were sent by Rodin. She even thought Rodin wanted to kill her. It sounds a lot like paranoid schizophrenia. Paul was shocked, and decided she was mad. Of course, looking at it another way, Paul might have been exaggerating. It was 1913 France, and this was the same brother who freaked when Camille moved out of the family home at twenty-two. Not that she wasn't in an altered state when he found her in her studio.

One book says it was her dysfunctional family that brought the insanity on. Her mother was cold, never hugged her children, while her father, who secretly sent money, was wild, imaginative and hot-tempered. Her mother loved Camille's sister, Louise, and maybe Paul, but not Camille. Mother and sister thought Camille was a disgrace, a whore. Actually, rethinking this, her brother was the only one in the family who understood her, worshipped her from the time they were kids. Wouldn't he be the best person to judge her mental state?

The whole thing is horrible. It's fucked. Who knows what therapy might have done—Freud was in his fifties then. Or meds. Camille berated people because they put her down for living by herself, for having cats as companions, for having what they called a persecution complex.

And there's a chance all her paranoia wasn't completely delusional. Strange things were happening with her art: one state commission was ditched mysteriously, and a museum piece was supposedly lost. And maybe Rodin actually was "stealing her ideas," by trying to harness her inspiration, her amazing talent, and by overusing her as a muse, draining her.

Oh my God. Camille . . . Cat.

No matter what the truth is about her sanity back then, she was vital to the heart of Rodin's creativity. It seems like her fierce competitiveness and her overwhelming anger at Rodin, for not marrying her, for abandoning her, for using her up, made her lose touch with herself in the end.

Fuck. It was so hard to look at it.

I turned to the last chapter of the book and read about her later years. The picture of her from that time was miserable, lifeless.

That's when Cat screamed beside me.

I could hear myself screaming, in a tiny wailing voice that trailed off out of my dream. *I saw an image of myself pacing in my studio, wild-eyed, then picking up a hammer . . . .*

My screams woke me, and I sat up straight. Someone's arms were around me.

It was Jesse. The shadows under his eyes looked darker. He was saying something.

"Cat, you must have had another nightmare. You're okay, you're okay."

We sat in silence. Then he spoke again, tenderly. "It's a tragedy what happened to Camille. It's really hard to deal with."

I nodded and leaned into him. "To me."

"To you. It must have been horrible. You were so talented, had such an influence on Rodin. And your anger . . . ."

"My fury, it swallowed me," I lowered my head.

"Cat, I hope like hell I can help you."

My sketchpad slid from my lap and landed on the gravel.

"Can I see your drawing?" he asked.

I retrieved it, and he turned it around until it was in the right position.

"That's beautiful. It reminds me of one of your marble sculptures from the past," he said, kissing my lips. "You know, I honestly think we'll both feel better if we get something in our stomachs." He gestured toward his automobile.

"*Oui*, I need to eat. That will help me find my way out of my memories."

He crossed the road, grabbed a bag from the front seat of his automobile, and set it beside me. Rummaging through it, he pulled out smoked salmon, romaine lettuce, capers, tomatoes, walnut bread, and finally, fresh peaches for dessert.

"How about here?" He laid out the dinner on one of the low round platforms in front of *The Gates of Hell*.

"A real feast," I said. When he crouched to put out the napkins, I ran my hands down the length of his spine.

"Dinner's ready," he said holding my hand and guiding me down onto the platform. We ripped off wedges of bread and made sandwiches, delighted with the exquisite tastes. When I was done, he brushed breadcrumbs from the side of my mouth. "So messy," he teased.

"I cannot help myself. It is delicious."

"You know, I can't do any more reading," he said. "I'm really beat. It's definitely enough for one night. How about you? Will you come with me to the car? We can just sleep."

"That sounds inviting, but can we have one last kiss out here?" I asked. "I need to sleep in the garden tonight."

"Really?"

"Really. I must. One more time."

"You know one thing I love about you, Cat? I can count on you to be completely unpredictable." He squeezed my side.

I licked his lip, bit it lightly, and kissed him firmly on his strong mouth. Then I placed a flower petal on my tongue and transferred it to his mouth. "Eat it and remember me in the aftertaste," I said.

"You sound so French tonight," he said.

"*Oui*," I said quietly.

"You know, I've got the early shift at work, so I won't wake you up in the morning. But when I get back, we'll need to do something special. Our last night here before we drive down south."

With his pack over his arm, he headed for his automobile, and I watched him—the shift of his hips, the hair falling on the back of his neck, the softness in his eyes when he turned back to look at me. My heart opened even more.

After scanning the garden from my old bench, I fell quickly asleep. When a dreadful nightmare woke me, I kept my eyes squeezed shut. The images from the dream were as clear as if they had just happened. They came from the darkest part of me, where I had buried them like a corpse that I would never touch again: *I saw myself in my studio. It was dark outside the windows, and no heat was left in the chilled, crowded room. The cats were mewing for food. I grasped a hammer from my tool shelf, and clenching it in my fist, I surveyed the room. Wildly, I began swinging it back and forth, digging into the plaster figures all around me, slicing, gouging out pieces of my own creations. I watched myself, features twisted into a silent scream, whacking at the heads and limbs of the statues that I loved, plaster in my hair and covering the studio floor, statues toppling and shattering on the ground. "You did this to me, Rodin," I shrieked. "You made me do this!"*

Half awake, half asleep, my eyes still closed, I stayed inside my nightmare. As my breathing quieted, more images appeared—of a woman, still and lifeless. I sat with the image for a while before I realized it was me: *I was sitting in a stark room, with a bed, a chair, and a small table. Inside an asylum. My uncombed mass of hair, bundled and clasped at the back of my head, was streaked with gray. I was writing to my brother, who had deceived me, committed me. An attendant stood in the doorway, holding a mound of red clay, but I was banishing him from my room. Once he left, I was alone, staring into space, eyes emptied of creativity, of curiosity. I had been there for a long time.*

My consciousness back in the garden, I clasped my arms around me to stop the violent shudders that followed. As waves of nausea passed through me, I drew my knees to my chest and clutched my stomach. I felt as if *The Gates of Hell* were inside me, burning me, destroying me, pulling me into a blackness with no end. I spiraled down, down, surrounded by it, whirling in it. It smothered me, choked me, suffocated me, until I was consumed by pain that seemed to have no end.

Until I saw a dab of light on the insides of my eyelids. Ever so slowly, like the dawn seeping cautiously into the night sky, the nausea began to lessen, the shudders began to ease their grip. The sun rose in the east and warmed me, calming my breathing. I faced the sun, my eyes still tightly closed, and dared to look back again at the images of myself the night I had wielded the hammer and rampaged against my own creativity.

This time, it was as if I were standing outside myself, watching with different eyes: *The hammer in my hand. My hair loosened from its clip. My eyes wild. Without judgment, I looked inside the woman I had been, who was destroying her beloved statues. I looked inside and found the desperation, the unquenchable fury at myself and at Rodin.*

I dared, too, to look once more at the ensuing years, from the time I was committed to the end of my life: *I saw myself again, a listless old woman, spending my days slumped in a wooden chair. I felt the despair and loneliness from decades behind the doors of the stark asylums I was not permitted to leave.*

I held all these feelings gently in my hands and watched them transform into a wide river of grief that overflowed my hands and swept me along in its wake. I found myself washed onto the banks of the river. And a deep compassion for myself rose up within me, like a tiny bud opening its petals. And with it came forgiveness.

I forgave myself for destroying my life with hate and blame, and for demolishing and driving away everything I had been passionate about.

I forgave my dear brother.

And, lastly, I forgave Rodin. He had wanted me only for himself—to teach and work with, to love, to gain inspiration from—but he could never commit to me alone. Truly, though, he did not mean to destroy me. He loved me as he could. He wanted me to succeed.

Mon dieu. In my last life, I did not lose a part of myself. I buried my hurt, my pain, my sadness inside me, as deeply as I could. Now I uncovered all of it and felt all of it. And found myself.

I reached out to myself in the past, and enfolded her in my arms. I stroked her hair, and rocked her. "It is okay. It is okay," I told her. I let myself cry as long as I needed to, until my past self and I merged into one person.

Inside, light crept through me, to every dark, damaged place, to every buried feeling, all the way to my core, and curled up like a cat in the sunlight. I felt more whole than I ever had, worthy of the warmth pulsing through me. Finally. A lifetime later.

I held myself until I was ready to let go, unaware of anything around me. When I finally opened my eyes, the sun made me blink at first, but then I could see it shining on my statue, *Meditation*, as it always did on clear mornings, but more brightly. I walked slowly toward the statue. This time, the seams in the bronze looked to me like the remnants of scars that had healed. I opened my arms to embrace the statue, but I instantly pulled them back, for the bronze was too hot to touch, as if it had been freshly cast in the night.

With a feeling that was both bitter and sweet, I knew what I needed to do. I looked toward the parking lot. Jesse had already left for the early shift at the grocery store. Near the arm of my bench, I found a blue flower with tiny petals and a tortoiseshell hair clasp that he had left for me. I kissed the clasp and pulled up the hair by my face, piling it on my head and fastening it, letting the hair in back hang loose.

I meditated for most of the morning. In the afternoon, I crossed the road and fashioned a rake out of branches fallen from the trees, tying the sticks together with long grasses. Back among the statues, I raked the gravel, up and back, only stopping when someone passed through. Up and back, up and back. It was soothing, even as sadness and joy interwove themselves inside me.

I passed the rest of the afternoon on and off in meditation.

*W*hen night fell, I entered the garden, holding the last page of my research paper and a grocery bag of food. Cat took my hand and led me to a bench.

"Thank you for the beautiful hair clasp."

"It looks amazing in your hair."

"Jesse, we need to have a talk." Her voice was more muted than usual.

"Okay, but I wonder if we should eat dinner first."

She covered my hand with hers.

"Please. I must talk to you now."

"Sure."

"Jesse, I love you so much. It is like a revolution for me—I could not be brave enough to love like this before, with so much hope and equality, and a lightness I have never known."

"Cat, what's going on? You sound different."

"I am different. I did something this morning that seemed to be impossible to do. It is only because my heart opened to you that I could do it."

"What do you mean?"

"In my dream . . . ."

"I think we should eat before you go on. You sound strange, and it's scaring me. Seriously."

"I do not think I can eat."

"Well, that's a new one." I tried to laugh.

"Really, Jesse. Something important happened. Please let me try to explain." She pulled my hand to her lap. "In my dream this morning, I could finally feel all the sadness I had hidden deep inside myself."

"That's great," I said, but I knew my expression didn't match my words.

"Next came forgiving . . . of myself in my past life. And of Rodin. You helped me do this."

"Cat. Forgiving sounds good, but please, stop just a minute. You don't sound like yourself. I'm not sure I want to know what you're going to say next." I stood up. "It's good we're leaving. You need to get out of here."

"Jesse, I . . . ."

"I know it'll take some creative thinking, but we can figure it out." I sat by her side, touched her hip, and lifted her leg over my leg, like the lovers of *The Kiss*. "Cat, I read the end of your story in my book. I know what happened. It's a lot to take in. Let's just take it easy."

We sat quietly, arms around each other. Then, she slid her leg off mine and touched the side of my face. "Jesse, something has changed."

Fear streaked through me.

"I need you to understand. I know it is not easy."

"I'll try to listen." I shifted on the bench so that I could look directly at her. I could hear myself breathing, as if I was inside myself.

"I know now that I have done what I was meant to do in this lifetime," she said.

"Then you can move on. We can move on . . . ."

"Jesse, it is time that you go to your new life in university."

"Right."

"And it is time that I . . . ."

"That you come with me."

Her voice was gentle, "That I return to my spirit self."

"Cat, you don't have to talk like this." My words resonated throughout the garden. I studied her, the blood rushing out of my face. "If you don't want to go with me, maybe we can find another way to be together. Or maybe you don't want to be with me at all."

"It is not true, Jesse. It is only that my time is . . . finished."

"Cat, listen to me. When things get resolved, it doesn't mean you have to go away. It can be a new start for us."

"Oh, Jesse, I wish I had power to change what is happening, but I do not." She hesitated and then spoke, in a hushed voice, "Jesse, the statue, it is burning hot again."

"Oh, God. Please. No." I put my face into my hands, and she stayed silent.

When I looked up, she was watching me, through tears. She kissed my cheeks and the backs of my hands. "I am so sorry, Jesse. I wanted, I hoped so much that I could stay with you."

"No." My shoulders sagged and I bent my head down.

She touched my arm and spoke again. "When people part, when we part, it does not need to be tragic. You can use our love for inspiration. You will create something from it."

"My God, this is so much bigger than . . . ." I looked at her and clasped her hands, trying not to hold too tightly. "Isn't there any other way? There must be."

"I wish it was so . . . but I know now why I came. It was to love you so much that I could become a person who knows how to forgive." She smiled, though her eyes showed her sadness.

A large moth flitted over one of the ground lights in the garden and landed on the armless shoulder of *Meditation*, flattened its wings, and rested there, waiting.

She shivered and pointed toward the moth. "It is time. The moth was here when I left the statue that first night."

"I remember your face that night," I said. "I was so messed up. I thought I was seeing things. It was just you and me in the garden. We were supposed to meet, for sure."

"*Oui*, Jesse."

I stood and pulled her up to me. I felt each point at which our bodies met, felt the love between us. We held each other, my arms around her neck, hers around my waist, until I felt her lightening her hold on me.

"You can let go, Jesse. It will be okay," she said.

"I'll try to let go . . . if that's what you need." I breathed deeply and slowly drew my body away from hers, my hands still touching her neck at first, then moving down to her arms, holding her hands, and releasing her fingers.

"Goodbye, my love," she whispered.

"Goodbye," I said, my voice shaking. "I love you."

She slowly turned to face *Meditation*. She took off her hooded sweater, and dropped it. She walked a few steps, pulled her lace top over her head, and dropped it. Her breasts shone in the moonlight as I watched her, still and silent. She took off her ballet shoes, her socks, her tights, and the ring on her toe, and left them in a trail as she walked across the gravel. Beads of sweat formed on her body, almost as if a fire was burning inside her. She stood there naked in the moonlight of the Rodin Sculpture Garden, then walked to the pedestal. The gravel crunched as I came to her side. From behind, I gently placed my hands on her waist, lifted her onto the pedestal, and stepped back.

I watched as she slowly transformed. Her skin became more porous and delicate, until I could no longer see the edges of her body, until she became a shape made of light. For an instant, I could tell that she could still see me, smiling at her with tears on my face. And then she became an amorphous form of tiny lights that multiplied and spread outward. They dissipated slowly, and when they were gone, I wasn't sure what I had seen. But I could feel her spirit filling the statue, then the garden, and beyond.

———— ♦ ————

When I could move again, I wiped away the tears from my cheeks and walked to the bench. I must have sat there for hours, because the night light changed around me. My body was encompassed by a feeling of emptiness and fullness. And an ache and a longing that deepened whenever I looked at the statue.

When I heard a car turning onto the road in front of the garden, I collected her clothes and tucked the silver toe ring into the blue sock. I set them on the bench and fumbled for the sketchpads she'd hidden underneath. Walking slowly, unsure of my footing, I placed all her belongings on the back seat of my car.

Returning to the statue, I said goodbye and touched its left thigh. It was no longer hot, not even warm. The white moth fluttered toward the ground light, and then upward into the darkness.

The crunch of the gravel was so familiar and so strange. The roar of my engine startled me enough that I could feel my body again, and the overwhelming longing in my chest. I reversed the car, then braked, reaching back for one of the sketchbooks and the blue sock. Placed them carefully on the seat beside me.

I drove down Palm Drive, past the spot where we danced. Down University Avenue, past the restaurant where we ate, and then merged onto the highway, heading south.

"I'll miss you," I said out loud.

I got myself from one green highway sign to the next, wiping at my eyes when I couldn't see well enough. I finally reached the first sign with double-digit mileage to Los Angeles.

In my mind, I saw her face again, her almond-shaped eyes, her lips, her long auburn hair. "You'll always be with me," I said. "But you're not my muse. I promise." The corners of my mouth momentarily flickered into a smile.

As I watched the sun replacing the moon, I fumbled with the blue sock, retrieved the ring, and slid it into the front pocket of my jeans. Then I eased into the center lane and headed for college.

Acknowledgments

Writing this novel required input and support from many people, of all ages, in different parts of my life.

Over many years, Robyn Russell edited the book and guided me in the revisions needed to make *Naked* work, from changing the structure and point of view, to pushing my characters where they needed to go, to my own use of language. She believed in the power of the story and the relationship so deeply that she kept this project near to her heart through it all.

My agent Amy Rennert encouraged me relentlessly during the long journey to write *Naked* and to find just the right publisher. Amy not only understands my writing, she supports me in every aspect of my life.

Camille Bocquillon, a young writer, editor, and translator outside of Paris, who friended me on Facebook, is integral to the success of this book. She was named after Camille Claudel, so it was a strange coincidence that we met while I was writing the novel. We became real friends, and her e-mails over the years, written in English by a French speaker, deeply informed the voice of Camille. She gave me insightful notes on the novel as well.

Thank you to Anna Halprin, and to her student and my friend, Tara Laidlaw, who invited me to "Dancing with the Rodins: Awaken," a dance program at the Stanford Rodin Sculpture Garden, that awakened the idea for this book.

Nick Godin is a consultant on all my novels, filling me in on what people really talk about and helping me develop the characters. John Beamer also helped in this regard, sharing deep insight into the character of Jesse. And Nathan Singer gave me tremendous feedback about the reactions of young men of Jesse's temperament.

My critique group members—Emily Jiang, Ann Manheimer, Marjorie Sayer, JoAnne Wetzel, and Caryn Yacowitz—were honest and insightful through endless revisions, and Kris Aro McLeod gave much-needed suggestions when I was stuck on the beginning.

Thank you to Melanie Chartoff, my improv teacher, who inspired the improv games in the book, and to my acting teacher, Kay Kostopoulos, and my acting-on-film teacher, Marty Pistone, who generously let me describe some of the drama exercises and filming techniques that they use in their classes.

I am grateful to Micaela Carolan, who taught me about Performance Art, along with my son James, who wrote a very helpful article about the subject in the *Wall Street Journal*. My son Dave gave me feedback on different versions of the story, over the years, and my son Tom, of course, lent his wonderful artistic talents to the book cover and the drawings of sculptures by Rodin and Camille.

Maria Damon always helps me find the truth in all my novels, as she did in this one, and she was my invaluable consultant on Iggy Pop.

Lastly, Camille Claudel inspired me deeply through her sculptures, her guts, her uncanny modernism . . . and her story.

A warm thank you to anyone I've inadvertently forgotten. So many people were vital to the realization of this novel.